TOYUK

THE MAKING OF A SHAMAN

J.PAULS

TERMINALLY COMMITTED TO CHRIST

Toyuk

CONTENTS

This has been a long journey. Many have been patient with me. First my wife Kathy, and my son Caleb, and my daughter Beth. My son has often urged me to write more throughout the years. As in any endeavor there are always those who come alongside and help.

This novel would not be here without the talents of Nathan and Robyn Hodgdon. Nathan's expert editing skills and Robyn's all encompassing tech and graphic skills which support all of my writing endeavors. They are my team. And I most definitely see them as extended family. I had a reading circle to read through the rough draft and give feedback. Ted Laurent, Brent Robinson, Doug Buettner, Kelsey Warnock, and my son Caleb. This novel sat for at least 30 years half finished in different forms. The last form was on a hard drive of a dead iMac. Thank you Jeff Vincent for yanking it out of the computer for me and saving me from retyping the entire thing. Even though the plot was complete and I knew all the steps loosely — I wasn't allowed to finish this story 30 years ago, even when I made several attempts at different periods in my life. Fast forward 30 years and with WAY more life experience and grey hair, I got multiple confirmations from many different sources that I was to finish this story. Several email conversations with Bill Myers were the final push I needed to obey. This has been a very long project and idea. But my Lord Jesus is a big proponent of 'story'. He kinda has a way with parables. The Holy Spirit took this story and gave me so many twists and turns and ideas that I definitely can not take credit for them. So many times I sat and asked Him, "Now what?" And the ideas flooded in. I often sat amazed. Many times I just became a recorder of the 'movie playing in my head'. So definitely I kinda became the co-writer to these long sessions of conversations with the Holy Spirit. Any glory or accolades should first go to Jesus, and His Holy Spirit, and then my team, and family and friends who all stood with me through this long process. I'm just trying my best to be obedient to His call. The Heavenly Father is always creative.

1

BOYHOOD LIFE

Sometime in the distant past, the sun rose over the peak of the rocky face, bathing the green mountain valley with gentle yellow light. The smoke of the morning cooking fires rose as thin, wispy trails in a still, quiet high Sierra valley. The tribe below had already begun its daily work. Women were preparing the morning meals. Children were slowly rising from their sleep. Men were discussing the needs of the day with other men. There was the hushed noise of morning rituals. It was another day in paradise.

Awakened to the smell of the cooking fires, Toyuk knew his mom was preparing his favorite breakfast. Toyuk stretched his arms and legs before sitting up to look out the doorway.

What a perfect morning for a swim, he thought to himself. He scrambled to his feet and rushed out past his mom down the trail to the river.

Mom called out to him, "Come back quickly or your breakfast will be cold!"

"I'll be back as fast as the hawk, mom."

Shushe smiled at her growing and changing son. *This year will be his year,* she thought to herself.

Toyuk reached the diving rock at the river and found that several other boys were already practicing their diving before a growing and admiring crowd of girls who just happened to be washing the breakfast utensils at an ever-slowing rate.

"Were you going to sleep all day?" Buldar yelled to Toyuk just before letting out his best warrior cry and diving off the rock. As Buldar came to the surface, there were giggles and laughter coming from the breakfast cleaning crowd.

"I was having those dreams again." Toyuk had scrambled his way to the very point of the diving rock as he spoke down to Buldar who was floating down the river on his back. Buldar and Toyuk had been almost inseparable in the past few weeks. Both had been working very hard on their skills so that they might be chosen for the manhood rituals this season.

Toyuk yelled at the top of his lungs and dove off the rock. Peals of laughter come from the cleaning crowd. Toyuk surfaced feeling so frustrated and embarrassed that he could not control the break in his voice. *I'm so tired of sounding like a girl*, he thought to himself. Buldar was busy scraping the water off his body when Toyuk came floating up to the bank.

"Don't give them the satisfaction, Toyuk." Buldar tried to console his friend. He was just thankful that his voice hadn't cracked before he dove. Toyuk gave Buldar a knowing nod as he rose from the cold river.

"A warrior needs his breakfast," Toyuk spoke over his shoulder to Buldar just before trotting back towards the breakfast fires.

Buldar called out, "Will I see you at the fishing hole this morning, Toyuk?"

"I'll be there."

Miccoon was the tribal elder who was in charge of the fishing ritual tests. His gentle ways and grandfatherly care made him a man whom Toyuk sought out very often. Toyuk was drawn to Miccoon and was thankful that he had someone he could talk to since he had no father to teach him the ways of the tribe. Miccoon was long past his warrior hunter days and was content to while away his hours at the river fishing. His skillful fishing provided much food for the tribe as well as provided him a high status in the tribe.

Toyuk and his mother had a low status in the tribe. Shushe's husband, Toyuk's father, was killed defending the tribe from a raiding party while Shushe was still pregnant with Toyuk. Their status in the tribe would have risen if Shushe would have become a second or third wife of another warrior, but the only offer came from the one-man Shushe could not stand, so she remained as a single mother in the tribe. She had the rights of the head of a family, but since she was a woman, she was the lowest in the tribal status hierarchy. Life was hard for Shushe and Toyuk. Shushe was hoping that if Toyuk could take his place among the warriors this year, their status in the tribe would surely rise.

Toyuk arrived at the fishing area Miccoon had set up for the manhood ritual testing. It was located in the curve of the river where the water slowed and left a large, shallow area shaded by the tree branches along the bank. Miccoon had staked an area and pulled a net around all of the stakes. He then had been catching fish and placing them into the netted area. The boys were to learn how to catch fish with their bare hands, learning how to slip under the fish with skillful, steady, and quiet hands while standing up to their knees in water. The trick was to learn the optical bend that the water caused in your line of sight and to maneuver your hands without scaring the fish.

Toyuk had listened and learned well from Miccoon and was by far the best fisherman among the boys. Buldar on the other hand needed all of the help he could get with fishing. He was good at running and shooting and even wrestling. Buldar could take down even the largest boy; he was strong, compact, and athletic. Toyuk was also good at running and shooting but was much thinner framed than Buldar.

"Haven't you caught one yet?" Toyuk shouted at Buldar as he arrived at the fishing testing area. Buldar was concentrating too hard to hear Toyuk's question. He was standing up to his knees in the water and moving with jerky motions. Miccoon just stood shaking his head while standing on the bank.

"He moves too much; he must learn to be more patient," Miccoon said in low tones to Toyuk as the boy took a place next to him sitting on a rock.

Toyuk sat looking out over the river. His eyes panned the valley and majestic mountain peaks. He could remember almost every tree and large rock in the valley. All of the boys were very familiar with their surroundings and never could have gotten lost, but Toyuk seemed to remember details and observe at levels better than anyone in the tribe.

Miccoon was acutely aware of Toyuk's gifts and abilities and marveled at the boy's understanding for one of his age. Miccoon felt a kinship with Toyuk and secretly kept his favorite place in his heart for Toyuk. Miccoon's only child died in childbirth and the event left his mate unable to bear any other children to her shame, and thus Miccoon had in his heart adopted Toyuk as a son even though the spread in years meant the boy most likely would have been his grandson.

Miccoon deeply loved his mate Ona, and never took a second wife. Toyuk had been welcomed into their lives and loved as their very own. Shushe and Ona spent most of their days working together, and they considered one another family. They shared most of the daily duties together and most meals were also shared. Ona was able to teach Shushe the intricate basket weaving she had learned from her mother. Ona's designs were the best in the tribe and were highly prized. The baskets would fetch a good value in trading.

"I've got one!" shouted Buldar, raising the wriggling rainbow trout in his hand.

"Good, now release it," said Miccoon while motioning Toyuk into the fishing area.

Toyuk slowly waded into the netted area. He stood still bent over with both hands in the water. In a few seconds he held a fish in each hand, to the smiling approval of Miccoon.

"Okay showoff, let's go to the shooting area." Buldar slapped Toyuk on his back.

"Just because it took you half the morning to catch one fish doesn't mean you have to take it out on me. Besides, I'll just beat you at that too." Toyuk was grinning out of the side of his mouth.

"That will be the day. The last one to the area has to retrieve all the arrows." And both boys were racing out of the river, splashing water everywhere.

The tribe was now busier than normal getting ready for the manhood and womanhood trials and ceremonies. Elders were in charge of the different testing areas. The best warriors and hunters would be the judges on whether the boys pass the challenges. The girls upon passing the womanhood ritual would be eligible for marriage, and many had already been promised to arrangements between families, but marriages had to wait until after the girl was initiated into the ranks of the women which took place the last night of the ceremonial week. Many of the girls and families were waiting until after the ceremony to make arrangements.

This was the case with Nea's family. Nea was a girl of Toyuk's age and the two had been friends for all of the years they had grown up, until the last year when in Toyuk's eyes Nea began acting strangely. Nea's father, Tregor, had high status in the tribe. He was the best hunter in the tribe and was the best inventor and builder of traps. Nea's beauty was quickly becoming noticed by all of the young men in the tribe, and the negotiations for her marriage were quickly becoming the talk of the women when such things were allowed to be discussed. Gossip and rumor flowed greatly around the possibilities of this year's ceremonies.

Nea's eyes had been there to watch the boys in the morning dive off the rock, and she was aware of how embarrassed Toyuk had been of his yell. She wanted to call out to him but thought it might bring more embarrassment to him, so she just stayed silent while the others laughed. She wanted to be closer to Toyuk, but every time she tried Toyuk seemed even more distant and aloof. She couldn't understand why he was so moody towards her.

Toyuk had begun to take a different notice of Nea. He was seeing her in a whole new light. His stomach for some reason always knotted up when she was around, and he could never say anything intelligent; his words all sounded stupid when she was near. So, to avoid any further embarrassment and pain, Toyuk had just begun to walk the other way when he spotted Nea coming. To his surprise, he began to fantasize what it would be like to have Nea as his mate. But this usually ended with Toyuk totally frustrated and telling himself that it would never happen. Nea comes from a family of high status, and the bidding for her marriage was already for the extremely wealthy only, he would remind himself. This vicious circle in his mind and heart caused Toyuk to push himself into many diversions that kept his mind and body busy and out of sight of Nea.

Buldar had noticed how much Toyuk was spending more and more time on the fringes of the village area. He didn't think much of it though since all of the boys were now working extremely hard getting ready for the trials.

"The best hunter is able to track one prey with an arrow while planning the next shot on another prey." Tregor was instructing the boys who were getting ready to practice their archery skills. Hoops were rolled twenty and thirty paces away in different directions and different paces while the boys tried shooting through the hoops with arrows. Tregor demonstrated by perfectly piercing three hoops as fast as he could draw back the bow. The boys were impressed, and even more determined not to let Tregor down when it came to their turn.

"Roll!" shouted Buldar, and three hoops began rolling at different speeds and distances. Buldar took aim and pierced two out of the three hoops with arrows.

"Very good, Buldar! I can tell you've been practicing." Tregor turned to Toyuk. "You're next."

Toyuk stepped up to the shooting line and shouted, "Roll!"

Just before the hoops rolled, Toyuk heard Nea call to her father. For a split second Toyuk's concentration was broken, but he refocused his mind and was able to pierce the furthest hoop. "Tregor, I can do better." Toyuk was now stepping back up to the line.

"You must learn how to push all distractions from your mind when you are in a hunt, Toyuk. Why don't you practice some more before coming back to the shooting field?"

Tregor was well aware of the distraction Nea had made on all of the boys on the field. He was also aware of the friendship that Nea and Toyuk had had. Tregor was now not at all encouraging to the friendship between his daughter and one of such low status this close to the ceremonial week, even though Toyuk had never given Tregor a reason to dislike him. Toyuk had also taken notice of how Tregor had recently been favoring others over him, and that Tregor always seemed to praise other boy's efforts more than Toyuk's.

After Nea was done speaking with her father, she approached the group of boys in which Toyuk and Buldar were standing.

"Toyuk, I would love to show you what I made for the ceremonial week; do you think you could come to see it tonight?" Nea smiled as her head tilted slightly.

"Uh—maybe, I have to see if my mom, I mean Miccoon needs my help with—uh—I don't know..." Toyuk kept staring at the ground making sure no eye contact could be made with anyone.

"Well, I would love to show you, Toyuk. I hope you can come." Nea smiled wide and turned to jog away.

"I think she likes you, Toyuk," Buldar spoke in low tones leaning into Toyuk.

"Hey, I wouldn't be messing with Nea, Toyuk, she's already been spoken for by Kinar."

"How would you know Leto?" Toyuk's face flared.

"Everyone knows Kinar will be doing everything in his power to secure Nea as a mate; you have seen how much he has been buttering up Tregor."

"Leto, you gossip like a girl. Go away." Toyuk turned to Buldar and said, "Let's go." Toyuk turned and walked away with Buldar following.

"You know what Leto said is true about Kinar trying to get Nea as a mate," Buldar spoke to Toyuk as they got away from the crowd.

"I know, I just don't like having it rubbed in my face by Leto. He is such a dung eater."

Buldar laughed. "Yeah, Leto does gossip like a girl." Now both Toyuk and Buldar laughed.

"Do you think Tregor will pass me on the shooting trials? You know how he favors everyone but me."

"You just concentrate when your turn comes – you'll pass."

"Do you think Kinar will be able to negotiate the deal with Tregor for Nea?"

"Kinar is the fastest and strongest warrior the tribe has, and he has not yet taken a mate," replied Bular, "and he has had his eye on Nea for some time now, Toyuk. Who can compete with him? And I'm sure Tregor is looking for every way possible to secure an even higher status for himself in the tribe. You know Tregor will agree as soon as he thinks he has gotten every gain out of Kinar that he thinks he can get."

"You're probably right, Buldar. I just think Nea will be miserable with Kinar. Kinar loves no one more than Kinar. He just wants Nea because she will look good for him...although I'm not sure who has the longer hair and is prouder of it."

"You better not say things like that when Kinar can get a whiff of it," Buldar said. "He'll squash you like a bug."

"I bet you could take him down, Buldar."

"I probably could, but then I would have to run faster than I ever have before and hope I had a big enough head start."

Both boys laughed, but Toyuk's insides twisted at the thought of Nea with Kinar.

At supper while Toyuk sat with Shushe, Miccoon, and Ona, his mind turned over the day's events and tried to wrestle them into making sense.

"Toyuk, how did you do today in practice?" Mom was probing for any words she could get.

"Fine." Toyuk grunted the one syllable word.

"He's definitely ready for the fishing test," replied Miccoon to Shushe. "And if he is doing as well in the other areas—there will be no question as to his readiness." Miccoon was truly proud and pleased with Toyuk.

"Sounds like I will have to prepare your tribal robes." Shushe had already finished his ceremonial outfit but didn't want Toyuk to know how much she wanted him to pass the initiation rite. Shushe put more food on Toyuk's plate and said, "Nea came by asking if you would come by to see what she has prepared for the ceremony. Will you go see her?"

"Maybe" came the monotone response.

"Hey Toyuk!" Buldar yelled as he ran up. "Aren't you done with supper yet? I was hoping we could practice our wrestling moves and get a few pointers from Growlon."

Growlon was Buldar's uncle and the elder in charge of teaching the boys hand-to-hand fighting. Growlon was known for his bear wrestling adventures, and had three grizzly claws hanging around his neck—one for each bear he had killed with his hands and knife.

Buldar was close to the best boy his age in wrestling but he wasn't the largest. The largest boy was Yellot, who was passed over last year when the manhood initiations were given. Yellot and Buldar always ended up in the finals of wrestling.

"Still trying to get one up on Yellot, aren't you?" Toyuk replied as he got up to join his friend.

The boys trotted off together to find Growlon at the meadow area.

"I hope that Toyuk will like what I added to his ceremonial coat," Shushe quietly said as she watched Toyuk run off with Buldar.

"I'm sure he will be very proud when he wears it on the final initiation evening. I would love to see what you have done, Shushe," Ona replied softly.

"Ona, could you share with me how you made the sun designs on Miccoon's ceremonial coat?"

"That is a great secret. I was hoping to pass that secret down to my daughter, but the Great Spirit has decided that I am not to have a child by my own flesh. You and Toyuk have become so close to Miccoon and me." Ona leaned in towards Shushe and spoke in a whisper, "I think Miccoon is planning on taking Toyuk as his son at the next New Year ceremony with your approval. I think he will be talking to you soon about the matter."

This was no surprise to Shushe, she could see the old man's heart had grown to treat Toyuk as a son. This would also raise the tribal status of Toyuk, but also leave Shushe in even a lower status because she would no longer be a head of a family. But she knew that Toyuk, once a fully recognized man within the tribe, would do everything in his power to take care of her and provide for her. If Toyuk passed the initiation rituals this year, Shushe had already decided to allow Miccoon to take Toyuk as his son.

"Don't you think the future son should look the part at his manhood initiation ritual ceremony?" Shushe still wanted the secret of Ona's sun designs.

"Maybe I can show you some plants to pick tomorrow," Ona said slowly with a wink and a smile.

The sunlight was fading and crept up the high stone cliffs surrounding the valley. Soft gentle breezes were blowing through the tops of the pines. The tribe was relaxing after the day's events except for the boys who were trying to be ready for the selection of the trials. The usual quiet of the evening was punctuated by the sound of boys yelling, grunting, and an occasional foot race through the camp area.

"Now, Toyuk, you must use your opponent's force to your advantage. As he lunges for you, use his thrust and execute the proper move." Growlon watched as Buldar and Toyuk circled one another in the soft grass. Both were waiting for the other to make the first move. In several places, boys faced off with each other as Growlon moved from area to area observing and advising boys.

"Come on, Buldar, give me your best move." Toyuk continued to circle to his right.

As Toyuk seemed to take his eyes off Budar, Buldar lunged towards Toyuk. Toyuk, who purposefully had looked distracted, nimbly stepped aside, grabbed Buldar from behind, and twisted him in midair. As they hit the ground, each boy fought their hardest to gain superiority and pin their opponent. In the end Buldar had Toyuk almost in a chokehold, when Toyuk slipped from his grip and stood up.

"You know I had you if this would have been the trials," Buldar said to Toyuk as both boys stood bent over panting with their hands on their knees.

Growlon came over to Toyuk. "Good takedown, Toyuk. Good reverse, Buldar. You boys are learning quickly. Enough lessons tonight. I'll see you tomorrow."

Both boys showed their respect to Growlon and left walking together back to the camp area.

"Let's go for a quick swim," said Buldar.

"The last one to the diving rock has to kiss a squirrel." replied Toyuk.

Both boys took off as fast as they could run. As usual Buldar would not admit to Toyuk that he had come in second when they got to the diving rock. It was the usual playful verbal sparring between the best of friends.

"Okay, Buldar, you can just kiss the rock where I dive off," Toyuk said just before jumping off the rock.

"Nice back flip, Toyuk, but if I kiss the rock, you have to eat grass. You lost in wrestling tonight." Buldar leaped from the rock in a high arc twisted one half turn and dove straight into the water. Both boys floated on their backs enjoying the cold river water.

The walk back to the camp area was slower than usual, as the boys were truly tired from the day's events.

"Do you want to come with me and have Miccoon teach you his special feather design for arrows?"

"Not tonight, Toyuk. I promised to recite our family history to my mother. She wants to make sure I get it correct for the trials. And my father is teaching me his arrow designs. I'll see you at the fire." Buldar gave a nod of the head as he turned to go in the direction of his family's dwelling place.

"Don't forget to kiss the rock!" Toyuk yelled.

"Don't forget to eat grass!" Buldar yelled back.

Both boys grinned unconsciously. As Toyuk turned he almost ran over Nea as she was walking up to him. They somewhat collided which left Toyuk very embarrassed.

"Will you come and see my ceremonial outfit, Toyuk?" Nea said gently with a smile.

"I didn't know it was your outfit you wanted me to see, Nea. Don't you think your father might not like me seeing you in it before the ceremony?" Toyuk drew in the dirt with his toe.

"I just wanted your opinion on a decision of what might go well as a headdress."

"I think you should ask your mother for that decision, Nea." Toyuk continued to look at the ground.

"Which do you like better, blue or red? Kinar has said he likes red, but I think blue will look better with my wrap."

Toyuk felt his hands go into fists at the mention of Kinar. Toyuk tried to speak softly, but his response came a little louder than he would have liked through his clenched teeth.

"Well, I think you should wear what you like, not what Kinar says."

"But I care what you think, Toyuk?"

"I think you shouldn't listen to Kinar," Toyuk said gruffly and then in a nicer tone made up an excuse. "I've got to go. Miccoon has asked me to help him tonight. Nea, you always look nice; I'll see you later." Toyuk quickly turned and walked towards his family's dwelling place.

"I hope we can talk some more tomorrow, Toyuk." Nea smiled as she turned to walk away.

The light of the day had retreated. Toyuk could see the tribe's communal fire beginning to blaze at the center of the camp. Families were already gathering sitting on blankets and logs in their groups around the fire. Toyuk headed towards where Miccoon, Ona, and his mother were sitting. Shushe had spread out a blanket, and she and Ona were working on leather garments. Miccoon had arrow shafts in one of Ona's baskets and was working on feather attachments.

"Come sit down, Toyuk. Let me teach you another way of placing feathers."

"What do you think the Shaman will be teaching us tonight?" Toyuk asked Miccoon as he found a seat next to the old man.

"Tonight he will explain the proper ritual after taking the life of the deer."

Ona leaned over to Toyuk and spoke in a low tone just above a whisper, "Are you still having those dreams? If you are, I would like to hear them again."

"I had another last night," whispered Toyuk in reply. Ona nodded. "They are very strange, I continue to see things I can't describe, I have never seen such things but in my dreams," Toyuk spoke to Ona in a low tone.

"Quiet, you two. the Shaman is beginning." Miccoon was focused on the Shaman who was dressed for the ritual.

The Shaman was wearing the full skin of a deer and carrying an antler piece in each hand. This was a time each year when the Shaman taught the stories and rituals which were important to the tribe. These times of teaching always came before the initiation rituals. The tribe looked forward to these times when everyone would gather to rehearse their beliefs and history. Many of the elders joined the Shaman in the teaching dances and stories.

Everyone enjoyed the evening of the Great Hunt. This story always involved members of the tribe dressed as many of the animals of the forest. The evening's events always ended with the men of the tribe heading towards the sweat lodge.

Those boys who were invited to the Manhood initiation trials looked forward with great anticipation when they would begin their sweat lodge rituals during the week of the testing.

This night the Shaman asked each of the boys who were going to be put through the testing to participate in the final hunt ceremony of the story. The hunter position, the most desired position by the boys, was given to Toyuk. With great flair and seriousness, Toyuk acted out the role. The entire tribe shouted joyously as the final "kill" was made, and all of the boys reveled in the attention. After the ceremony, the tribe slowly left for their respective sleeping areas.

Miccoon leaned into Toyuk. "Good job tonight, son." The emotion was thick in his voice.

"Thank you, Miccoon. Hopefully I will be able to do it for real next week."

"You'll do fine." Miccoon turned and walked with Ona to their sleeping area.

"You know Nea was really watching you, Toyuk."

"Yes, mother, everyone was watching me. I was the hunter tonight."

Toyuk was ready for sleep, but he was wondering if his mind would let him. So much was swimming in his head. Toyuk wished for a dreamless night's sleep. His dreams of late were so disturbing and unusual.

2

THE DREAM

Toyuk's sleep that night was not peaceful. His dream was filled with places and things he had never seen before. He was constantly running and hiding in his dream; he was terrified. The people in his dreams were not even dressed like anyone he had ever seen. Toyuk thought he was in another world and didn't know how to get out. He was always looking for an escape but never finding it.

"Toyuk, wake up." Shushe was gently nudging his son. "You're having a bad dream."

Toyuk jolted awake and sat up, breathing hard, his body drenched in sweat. It was still pitch black in their small shelter.

"It's okay, Toyuk. I'm here." Shushe was stroking Toyuk's hair and speaking in low, comforting tones.

"I was having the dream again," Toyuk said while letting out a frustrating sigh.

"You know Ona would like to help you, if you would just share it with her."

"I don't even know how to describe what I am seeing." Toyuk replied. "Everything in my dream is so different, and the people even speak a different language."

"Why don't you try to talk to Ona? She won't make fun of you; you know how much she respects your gifts from the Great Spirit."

"This dream doesn't seem like any gift, more like a curse!" Toyuk said with increasing volume and anger. He realized his voice was getting too loud and whispered, "I will talk with her tomorrow."

"Maybe a good walk will calm you." Shushe knew Toyuk needed to have time to settle down. "I'll be fine, you go for a walk."

Tuyok got up, and pushed back the skin, and walked out into the cool night air. He could see the embers from the tribal fire and turned to walk towards the river. He looked up and saw the moon was just a sliver now and close to the horizon; soon, when it was new, the ceremony time would begin.

The air was still and cool. The trees made no sound as Toyuk walked the path towards the river. The stars were bright, and the rushing of the river soon drowned all other sounds out. Toyuk made the way to a large rock next to the river, climbed on top, and sat leaning back on it.

His thoughts were turned toward the Great Spirit. His mother's comment about gifts had him wondering if the Great Spirit really was trying to communicate with him somehow. *Funny way of trying to communicate with me if I don't understand any of it!* Toyuk thought to himself. His mind was now racing with thoughts about the Great Spirit and everything he had heard from his mother, Miccoon, Ona, and the tribal evening fires. He thought of the feelings he got when recalling how the tribal Shaman spoke of the Great Spirit. A cold chill ran down his back.

The Shaman always made one fearful not to evoke the Great Spirit's wrath. The Great Spirit, the way the Shaman described him, made Toyuk feel very far away from him and that he was but an ant that could be squashed if he made the Great Spirit angry at him. But the way Ona spoke of the Great Spirit, she seemed to make him feel like the Great Spirit was one who you could actually talk to and learn from. Toyuk's feelings were confused and his mind was filled with disjointed thoughts. Finally, he felt like he would just do it. He gathered up his courage and began to speak out loud.

"Great Spirit, if you are listening—please explain what my dream means... is it from you? I don't know if you can hear me or not—but I ask for your help; show me what I need to do, teach me what I need to know. I want to know you and your ways. Help me know you."

The only sound Toyuk heard was the river. But in his heart, as he felt a peace beginning to grow, he knew he had done the right thing asking for the Great Spirit's help. He wondered if he should also ask for some of the other spirits' help that the Shaman had taught about. His feelings did not always sit well with the teachings from the Shaman, but he didn't know why, and he figured he would leave it as is. *Why would anyone deal with any other spirit if you could deal directly with the Great Spirit?* Toyuk thought to himself. He then remembered some of the things Ona had said and remembered how Ona and the Shaman didn't always get along.

"Tomorrow I will speak to Ona, even if I can't describe what I see in my dream," Toyuk heard himself say under his breath as he climbed off the rock to walk back to his shelter.

The next morning after the swim at the diving rock, Toyuk broke away from Buldar and went in search of Ona. He found her with the other women at the grinding rock. Toyuk didn't approach the rock but stayed a good distance away in the line of sight of Ona. When Ona looked up, she saw Toyuk standing near some trees and excused herself from the group. Once she got up, Toyuk started for the river where Miccoon was teaching fishing and then turned towards the meadow. When Ona came to the meadow, Toyuk was sitting on a log. They were the only ones that could be seen in the meadow. Ona sat on the log and waited for Toyuk to speak first.

"I guess my mom told you about last night." Toyuk said hesitantly.

"She told me you were having the dream again."

"I don't know where to begin... so many things I do not understand are in the dream, they don't even speak our language, and it is all so different."

"Tell me what you can," Ona said, "and I will pray that the Great Spirit will give me understanding."

Toyuk wondered if he should tell Ona about how he had prayed to the Great Spirit the night before, but told her of his dream instead. "My dream always begins with me running away, no – running to something. Oh, I don't know which it is, maybe both. Anyway, I am running, then everything goes black and then the light comes, and everything is very strange, and people dressed funny and talking another language come and probe me and stick me. I try to get up but there is something like flat ropes holding my hands and feet to the thing I am laying on. I can't get off no matter how hard I try. And sometimes I dream of being in a very big shelter which has many rooms with other people who also dressed funny and very pale but different from the first people and they are speaking to me in the strange language and then I hear myself speaking to them in their language. They seem friendly to me, but I don't know. I see things I have no way of describing to you, things that move faster than a horse or even an eagle on the ground with people inside of them like they don't mind being eaten by them and carried away. I've seen very small pale people in a closed basket with a window talking. I've seen birds so big and flying very high that never flap their wings, soaring like an eagle but never turning. I have seen more people in one place, like equal to summer trading time but it seems like it is that way always. So many pictures I cannot describe, but I almost always feel scared yet there is a knowing that I am there, or will be there, oh I don't know."

Ona remained silent waiting for a time for Toyuk to go on if he chose to.

"I guess I want to know why I am being shown these things, it is so confusing and frustrating and exciting all at the same time, yet I don't know what I need to learn from it. Can you help me, Ona?"

"So many strange things, I believe you, Toyuk, that you are having this dream, and I believe that the dream is from the Great Spirit. I believe the Great Spirit is preparing you, Toyuk, for a great journey. I don't have anything else to tell you, but I will pray that the Great Spirit will help me guide you in the way you should go." Ona hesitated before asking the next question, "Have you asked for the Great Spirit's help?"

"Yes." Toyuk thought of saying more but let the silence linger. "Please don't tell anyone else."

"Things from the Great Spirit are sacred and not to be shared unless it is from the one who received it from the Great Spirit. I will not share this with anyone, even Miccoon. It is for only you to share." Ona bowed her head as she talked.

"Ona, should I be consulting the Shaman and asking for the other spirits' help?"

"You may tell anyone you feel you need to, but I don't think that Rohue will be able to tell you more. He always makes others fearful of the Great Spirit, and I don't feel that the Great Spirit is a mean and terrible Spirit, but One who cares for His creation. Rohue will just want you to perform some ritual that will cause you to owe him in some way, keeping you coming back to him for all the answers and the next steps. He has many in this tribe running so many circles that they almost don't have time for anything else and he is getting rich off of them. Besides, I don't think Shushe could afford one of his consultations right now. I believe, Toyuk, that you are right in keeping this to yourself. Let the Great Spirit guide you, as to the other spirits – aren't they less than the Great Spirit? Seek the Great Spirit's help above all." Ona sat silent making sure that Toyuk was the next to speak. Ona had taken a great chance with Toyuk by not speaking highly of Rohue.

"Thank you, Ona, for listening to me." Toyuk got up to leave and as he walked away, he turned and whispered to Ona, "I agree with you about Rohue – and don't worry, we never had this conversation." Toyuk knew that Ona had taken a great risk, but so had he in speaking to a woman about spiritual matters, so they both had their reasons to remain quiet about the subject.

Ona smiled to herself and thought that Toyuk might make a great Shaman one day. *Is that your plan for Toyuk, Great Spirit?* she prayed and questioned silently as she scanned the opposite towering ridge of the Sierra valley. Ona got up and slowly made her way back to the communal grinding stone, her mind filled with Toyuk's dream.

Toyuk still wrestled with his thoughts and emotions and began to run the trail that led up the side of the valley. He didn't know why but he began to feel angry which spurred an even faster pace up the trail. Toyuk did not stop until he had reached the rim of the canyon overlooking the valley above the tribe's summer camp. From the lookout the view was majestic, and he could see the entire valley and mountain ranges beyond. He sat down on a rock, which gave him an unobstructed view of his entire surroundings. As Toyuk scanned the view before him he thought about his life, trying to make sense of all the recent changes that had been happening to him, the relationships that were changing and how he fit into them, his body and voice changes and his desire for them to come quicker and be over, and his inability to understand the dreams he had been having. Toyuk stayed on the rock and began to pray out loud to the Great Spirit, telling Him all of the things on his mind. After he had exhausted everything, he could say he began to feel a peace come over him. It was late afternoon when Toyuk began the trek down the mountain. When Toyuk reached the camp, Buldar came running up to him.

"Where have you been all day?"

"I was up on the mountain—thinking."

"Well, you missed all the final instructions from the elders on the different challenges we will have to pass." Buldar was visibly frustrated with Toyuk.

"So, will the choosing ceremony be tonight?"

"I think everyone believes it will be, but you know how the Shaman is. He waits until the last so that everyone and all of the attention will be focused on him, but everyone is making ready for the ceremony tonight. Come on, your mom has been waiting for you." Buldar grabbed Toyuk and the boys began to walk towards Toyuk's and Shushe's shelter.

"Come, Toyuk, and have some fresh fish." Shushe had prepared a meal that caused the rumble in Toyuk's stomach growl all the more.

"Yes, Buldar, there is enough for you too." Shushe smiled at the wide eyes both boys had as they were eyeing the food. Both boys looked like wild dogs as they began to stuff the food into their mouths. "Slow down, we have plenty of time before the Shaman announces the ceremony plans." Shushe was smiling at the boys as they continued their ravenous eating. "Are you sure, Buldar, that your mom knows that you are having supper with us?" Shushe spoke with some concern.

"Oh, she won't miss me. I'm sure my younger brother and sisters have already eaten my portion."

"You be sure that you tell her that you were invited to have dinner with us tonight." Shushe was talking with all motherly concern.

"I will, Shushe. Your fish is always so good! How do you make it?" Buldar asked with a half-full mouth of fresh trout.

"You know better than to ask a woman for her cooking secrets, Buldar. Do you like the cakes?" Shushe was known for her sweet corn cakes. They were the size of a thick pancake.

"That's obvious, mom; he is on his fifth one." Toyuk was thoroughly enjoying his supper and it was obvious from all the humming sounds coming from Buldar that he was too.

Miccoon had his arm around Ona as they were walking towards the three having supper. "So, are you boys ready for tonight?" Miccoon was grinning as he looked at the boys.

"The Shaman hasn't made the announcement yet, has he?" Buldar said as he reached for another sweet corn cake.

"Oh, it will be tonight, don't worry. Toyuk, are you ready?" Miccoon spoke directly and firmly to Toyuk.

Toyuk looked at Miccoon. "I believe that the Great Spirit has made me ready, as well as from the wisdom and help from all of the elders, yes, I am ready."

Ona smiled and remembered her thought of Toyuk becoming a Shaman, thinking that he was even beginning to sound like one.

"Look, the elders are gathering everyone together." Shushe was looking towards the communal fire ring area.

"The time has come. Come, Ona, let's find a good seat. " Miccoon and Ona strolled away.

"Come on, boys, finish up. I need to do a few things before tonight. You boys go without me and find a place next to Miccoon and Ona, would you, Toyuk?"

"Yes, mother."

"Thank you for supper, Shushe. It was delicious!" Buldar was already on his feet and beginning to walk backwards as he spoke. He turned to run towards his family's shelter and waved in reply to Shushe's yell.

"You're welcome, Buldar!"

Shushe headed into their shelter as Toyuk began to walk towards the ring. Shushe quickly got out the hidden ceremonial tunic she had been working on for Toyuk and placed it in her clothing, and the one item she had been saving for this time that Toyuk knew nothing about before she headed towards the ring herself. She was full of emotions, feeling the loss of her little boy, excitement that he was becoming a man, fearful of the dangerous trials he would be facing, and joyful of the honorable and capable man Toyuk was becoming. Her eyes began to fill with tears as she walked, her mind racing through a thousand memories of her cherished little boy. Tonight meant a whole new season of life was beginning for Toyuk and her.

3

THE CHOOSING CEREMONY

The drums were sounding as the tribe was being called to the communal fire ring. Toyuk arrived before Miccoon and Ona and had taken the usual family spot around the ring. Toyuk watched as Buldar and his family arrived and sat down at their usual position. Toyuk very slightly nodded at Buldar, as Buldar closed his eyes returning the recognition by Toyuk.

Other families were now taking their places around the ring. Miccoon and Ona had arrived, smiled, and sat next to Toyuk without saying a word. There was a general hush among the tribe as they gathered which marked a great difference to the usual noise of the communal ring. Everyone was waiting for the Shaman to appear and announce this evening's agenda. The tribe was about to take dramatic changes, and everyone could feel the anticipation.

The drums began to beat faster and faster until they all stopped at once. The silence was deafening. A large single, shrieking cry seemed to come from all around them and then the Shaman appeared at the center of the ring. The Shaman under his cloak began to point his finger around the circle to various members while beginning to talk in hushed tones.

"Tonight, our tribe will name those called to take on the change." As he said "the change" all of Toyuk's hair seemed to stand on end.

"Tonight... those called will begin their vow of silence. Tonight, we will know who is called to become part of the tribe, but the spirits will choose who is worthy." The Shaman seemed to say the word "choose" with an unearthly quality that left everyone uneasy.

Toyuk felt Miccoon's hand on his shoulder. Toyuk turned and looked at him and was glad for the old man; his hand seemed to calm his nerves some. Miccoon smiled confidently and could feel the tenseness in Toyuk's body slowly relax.

Everyone seemed to look at one another after hearing the word "choose" spoken by the Shaman, but when they looked back to the center of the circle, the Shaman was gone.

The tribe's chief slowly rose from his seat and walked to the center of the ring. He spoke in a loud, authoritative voice. "Let the council of elders stand with their chief."

One by one men began to get up and join the chief at the center of the ring. Toyuk understood as the third man rose to join the chief that they were rising by status. Miccoon suddenly rose. Toyuk looked up at Miccoon startled and then watched the old man join the elders in the center. Of course, Toyuk knew that Miccoon would be getting up, but somehow as the old man rose Toyuk had a much deeper understanding than he had ever had before about the whole of tribal responsibilities and status and that now he might be joining that group someday. Toyuk watched with a new type of love at Miccoon. He felt proud and humble at the same time. So many emotions were awakening in Toyuk that he struggled to keep the moisture in his eyes from becoming noticeable.

Just as Toyuk became aware that his mother had not yet arrived at the ring he saw her out of the corner of his eye carrying a bundle under her arm. Shushe sat down next to Toyuk as the elders began to call out the names of the boys that would be named this year for the ceremony.

"Buldar, son of Budar."

"Yellot, son of Wisman."

"Leto, son of Goew."

"Toyuk, son of Tonuw"

Toyuk was not used to hearing his father's name, so he was somewhat startled when he heard his name called. He scrambled to his feet and joined the other boys whose names had been called. All in all, there were ten boys who had been called, which was no surprise to the tribe—unlike last year when Yellot had been passed over.

"Everyone knows that from this time forward that the 'called' must keep the vow of silence until their trial is over 3 days from now. Let us help them by not talking to them." The Chief was saying something that all of the adults knew, but it was said mainly for the boys' younger siblings. And after the Chief's instructions, parents could be seen reminding their younger children not to engage their older brothers.

"You may now give the 'called' their initiation bundles."

After the Chief made the last statement, fathers of the boys began to rise and bring bundles to the boys. Shushe got up and went to Toyuk. Toyuk knew that his mother had been working on his initiation bundle but had never been able to catch her working on it. Shushe handed Toyuk his bundle, smiled at her son, with tears in her eyes she walked back to where she had been sitting.

Toyuk felt something hard in the bundle which he did not expect. He couldn't wait to look at the contents. But there would be time this evening. The boys now formed up in single file to walk to the area which had been prepared for them some distance away from the normal living areas. Toyuk thought of Nea as he walked and knew that the girls would be called out after the boys had gone. He fought with his emotions and feelings. He wanted to see her in her ceremonial outfit, but knew that would be too distracting to him and he needed to concentrate on the upcoming trials. Maybe he should have gone to see her outfit before the ceremony as she had asked. His thoughts kept coming back to Nea, and he kept pushing them from his mind.

Toyuk thought to himself, *I must keep focus*.

The boys were now walking up the side of the canyon in the dark. When the boys arrived at the prepared place, they quickly chose their sleeping areas and began pushing pine needles together for their beds. All was silent as the boys began opening their bundles. One of the elders had already started a fire and prepared a hot ritual drink for the boys. The liquid was bitter to the taste but Toyuk could feel his body relaxing.

"Quickly open your bundles; you will be sleeping shortly," the elder said somewhat shortly to the boys.

Toyuk opened his bundle to find a new tunic, which had very colorful and intricate designs. Toyuk could tell that Shushe had had help from Ona, because the designs were masterful. Something fell out of the tunic when he opened it. It was a large obsidian knife with a carved deer antler handle and a leather sheath. The name was on the sheath was Tonuw. Toyuk inspected the knife carefully; he had never seen it before and wondered where his mother had kept it all these years. It was very sharp and Toyuk had not seen one like it in all of the tribe. He wondered what his father must have traded to receive such a highly prized weapon.

Some of the other boys noticed the knife Toyuk was inspecting, and there were many wide eyes as well as some jealous ones as they watched Toyuk turn the knife over in his hands. Buldar wished he could speak to Toyuk to ask him about the knife, but the code of silence was one he was not about to break; the trials had just begun.

Toyuk also found in his bundle some arrows obviously made by Miccoon, and some rope that was coiled and intricately woven. He could tell the rope would hold his own weight if needed.

Toyuk's thoughts raced through his mind as he lay down on his pine needle bed. *What would the next three days be like? What did Nea look like in her ceremonial outfit? Would Kinar be next to her?* Toyuk felt hot anger, but his mind kept on racing. *Where did his father get the knife? How come his mother had never shown it to him? I wonder if I am going to have that dream again?* Toyuk felt himself falling into the darkness of sleep, *what was in that liquid anyway?* By now the liquid had taken effect and all of the boys were sleeping soundly.

Back at the tribal ring, the girls were now being called out. The Chief was calling out their names. After four names were called came Nea's name.

"Nea, daughter of Tregor."

Nea jumped from her place and ran to where the other girls were standing. After all of the names had been called, there were sixteen girls in the center of the ring. One could tell the girls were extremely excited, yet everyone marveled on how quiet they could all be.

"You may now bring the 'called' their initiation bundles." Mothers now rose and began handing bundles to their daughters. Many mothers began sobbing as they went back to their places.

"Fathers, you may now bless your daughters."

Fathers began to rise and walk to their daughters. Some fathers put their right hand on their daughters' heads while speaking a blessing over them, while others preferred to hug their daughters while they said their blessing. Mothers cried all the harder as their husbands returned to their seats.

The girls then began to walk single file to their prepared place just adjacent to the tribal living area next to the river. The girls were to stay in the tribe's largest dwellings specially made for this time of season.

The night had been completed. The people of the tribe began to break up and walk back to their dwellings. Shushe felt very alone as she walked back to her dwelling, and she wondered if she would be able to sleep tonight.

4

THE TRIALS

The fishing trials were the first to be accomplished. Buldar had barely passed, and Toyuk had come in first with the largest fish in the shortest amount of time. This trial was not like the practice area, for the nets had been taken down and the boys had to fish in the river with no kind of help. Miccoon had already spent considerable time with Toyuk fishing and Toyuk knew where all of the best fishing holes were.

The archery trial was the one that Toyuk was nervous about. Tregor was barking orders to the boys, and the boys were scrambling to follow the orders as fast as possible. Toyuk settled his mind and forced himself to concentrate, pushing everything from his mind. This time not all of the rings were on the ground rolling; some were swinging from tall trees and released at different times. The boys had a chance to pierce five rings of different sizes at different times, different speeds, and different directions. Each boy had to be very still, listen, and concentrate to hear where the next ring was coming from. When his time came Toyuk moved with determination and was able to pass the test. Five rings passed by, and Toyuk was able to pierce four. Toyuk so wanted to encourage Buldar as his friend stepped up to the shooting circle, but by now all the boys had adapted to the silence code. Toyuk found himself thinking and tossing up thoughts to the Great Spirit throughout the day, for the Great Spirit to help him focus and to help Buldar pass the trials. Toyuk found himself surprised how much he began to think about the Great Spirit and how much he began to ask for His help.

The wrestling trial ended with Buldar actually besting Yellot with a lightning-fast reversal at the end. Toyuk had lost to Yellot in the last round when he couldn't bring Yellot down. Gowlon praised Toyuk's efforts, telling him that he had passed the trial but needed to be more patient when facing such a large foe. Leto faced the humiliating fact of being in last place and was in danger of not passing the wrestling trial; his fate was left in Growlon and the other elder's decisions. Leto left the trial area not knowing if he had passed.

The next trial was one the boys were not expecting. They were challenged to throw stones at targets running from target area to target area. Some targets were pine cones, while some were wooden figures sitting on rocks. The boys had to stay behind trees until their name had been called. None of the boys were allowed to see the course before their time. Most of the boys were able to pass the test, but Yellot had difficulty because his eyes weren't as sharp as most of the boys; he preferred targets that were closer. Buldar and Toyuk flew through the course and tied for second place behind Leto who had surprised everyone with his rock throwing skills.

By this time of the day the boys were sweaty and dirty, and the sun was heading towards the horizon, when Growlon told the boys to go wash in the river and report to their sleeping area. The boys ran to the river and jumped in, so relieved that the day was almost over. Miccoon didn't allow the boys any time for enjoyment of the river. He quickly told them time was up and they needed to report to the sleeping area. All the boys were ready for a big meal and wondered if they would get any food, for they had not been given any breaks for breakfast or lunch. When they arrived at the sleeping area a new circle had been formed around the fire pit, and to their disappointment there was no food in sight. Growlon instructed the boys to face away from the fire, be at least an arm's length from any other person, and to sit cross-legged. Tregor then instructed the boys to close their eyes and visualize each of the trials they had been through. The boys were instructed to find their errors during the trial and to visualize what they could do to correct the problems and to visualize them doing it right the next time.

Toyuk focused hard on each trial in his mind. Step by step he saw himself in each part of each trial, making mental notes where he could have done better and then seeing himself doing the trial with no flaws or mistakes. His stomach was growling, as were all of the stomachs of the other boys, which made their concentration very difficult. Every boy wanted to speak out about being hungry, but no one was willing to break the code of silence for fear of not passing the initiation.

After a time, the elders told the boys to rise and follow them. The men walked down next to the river where the boys were told to take off all of their clothes and were ushered into a small sweat lodge. The lodge was made up of large pieces of bark leaned together in a conical fashion. Hot stones from a fire just outside the lodge were placed in the center of the lodge where an elder poured water over them, creating steam that filled the tiny lodge. The boys were so close together and the heat was almost unbearable. When the elders said the boys could visit the river, they tumbled out of the lodge in such a hurry that many boys passed out when they stood up and fell in the dirt.

Miccoon told the boys to go slow, as the sweat lodge was also a trial to teach them about their bodies and their limits. The elders made sure to turn the boys who fell onto their backs, warning them not to get up too quickly. After a quick dip in the river, the boys went back into the sweat lodge. This procedure was repeated three times. After the third time, the boys were told to get dressed and report to their sleeping area. Again the boys' hopes of food were dashed; nothing had been prepared. They all went to their sleeping mats extremely hungry and were asleep almost instantly.

The next morning the elders got the boys up early, and again there was no breakfast provided except for cold water to drink. Today the boys would have to create a usable bow, three arrows, and one throwing spear. The boys already knew that these weapons would be used in their final trial, and that their skill of creating good, usable weapons would have a dramatic impact on their ability to do well in the next few days. The boys all went in different directions to gather the needed raw materials.

Miccoon had already shown Toyuk where there was good raw stock for creation of a bow and arrow, and Toyuk had already scouted a tree from which he would use a limb for a spear. The day was spent gathering, cutting, carving, and tying. Toyuk was surprised how much easier the job was made by using his father's knife rather than the small blade he was used to. The blade was sharp and the whittling and carving went very fast. By the end of the day, Tuyok was satisfied by the weapons he had made; they were crude but they were usable.

Buldar was still fighting with getting his spear made when Toyuk came over and handed him Toyuk's father's knife. Buldar nodded with a big smile and went at the spear with a new purpose and speed. In a very short time Buldar was reverently handing the knife back to Toyuk with a nod and shake of the head.

Toyuk understood Buldar's face; yes the knife was something very precious.

The day ended again with a trip to the sweat lodge. The boys, extremely hungry, plodded down the path to the river. Standing before the sweat lodge stood the Shaman wearing a bearskin that covered his complete body and head. The boys were instructed to take their clothes off and line up.

The Shaman called each boy to him, handing him something to chew while in the sweat lodge. As each boy entered, they quickly began to chew on the item. This time the lodge filled with steam, heat, with elders chanting just outside the walls. Drums were beating as the chants rose and fell in different intensities. The boys were told to allow their spirits to go where they needed to go.

Toyuk felt very different then he had ever felt, and he knew the item he was chewing on was causing him to see things that weren't there. He didn't know how to interpret what he was seeing; again came images from his dreams. He wanted to run but his body wouldn't move. This time the images were filled with people who were not friendly, and had creatures on their backs who were riding the people. The creature's faces were hideous and scowled at Toyuk, sometimes trying to reach out and grab Toyuk as the people came near him. Toyuk found himself crying out for the Great Spirit's help, but only garbled sounds came out of his mouth. By now most of the boys in the sweat lodge were making noises no one could understand. The images Toyuk was now seeing in his hallucinations were different from his dream in that the people now had terrible, hideous creatures on their backs and were mean. As Toyuk cried out to the Great Spirit the people and creatures were driven back, with the creatures slapping their claws over their ears every time Toyuk called out for the Great Spirit. Slowly the images were fading and Toyuk found himself outside of the lodge lying on the ground, face up with cold water being splashed onto his face. He didn't have any sense of how long the experience had lasted, and was thankful to be allowed to wash off in the river.

After returning to the sleeping area the boys were told by the Shaman to sit and close their eyes, going over the images they experienced in the sweat lodge. Toyuk didn't want to revisit the images but remained silent and began to ask questions of the Great Spirit in his mind. *What were those terrible hideous creatures?*

"*Spirits,*" came the reply to his mind.

Startled, Toyuk quickly opened his eyes. He thought someone near to him had spoken the answer. Slowly looking around, he didn't see anyone that could have said the word to him. "*Great Spirit, was that you?*" Toyuk asked in his mind.

"*Yes,*" came the reply clear and strong in his mind.

"What are my dreams about?"

Silence.

"*Will you speak to me and teach me what I want to know?*"

More silence.

"*What do you want me to do?*"

"*Learn of me,*" came the reply in the form of a whisper in Toyuk's mind.

"*What do you want me to learn?*"

Silence.

"*Will you speak to me some more?*"

The Voice would not say another word. Toyuk began to wonder about the answer given to him that the creatures were spirits. Did this mean that the Great Spirit was like those hideous, terrible creatures but only larger? The moment he had that thought, the voice boomed in his head, "*I am that I am! Those creatures are fallen spirits cast from my Presence. Do not worship any spirit but the Great Spirit. Do not seek wisdom from any spirit but the Great Spirit, for I am that I am.*"

Toyuk was stock still, not wanting to move, not wanting to do anything but put his face flat on the ground. Toyuk felt a Presence he had never felt before; he felt small and scared. His mind raced, *was this real*? *Is it possible to actually converse with the Great Spirit and live?* Toyuk remained with his face to the ground for a long time. The Presence left him and he opened his eyes wondering if the experience had been real. It had to be; the item he had chewed was long gone, he realized. He slowly rose from the ground, made his way to his sleeping mat, and found all the boys were already on their mats asleep. He fell asleep, turning the entire conversation with the Great Spirit over and over in his mind.

5

NEA'S ACCIDENT

The morning broke with warm sunshine and birds singing. The girl's initiation area was alive with activity, almost a complete opposite of the boy's site. The girls were not held to a code of silence or given trials to complete. Fasting was certainly not happening in the girl's area, for each elder woman was teaching special recipes to the girls while the girls each took turns cooking the meals and were provided all the ingredients necessary. Their time was one of bonding and learning from other elder women from the tribe and with each other. So many girls living together all excited about marital prospects and thoughts of starting a family made for a very lively bunch. There was their share of disputes and jealousies, but for the most part the elder women kept everything in line.

Nea was considered one of the most envied because of the rumor about Kinar asking Tregor about marital bargaining issues. There were lots of giggles and whispering whenever the name Kinar was brought up. Nea tried not to let all of the attention get to her; she enjoyed the spotlight but didn't like being talked about in hushed circles behind her back. Every now and again her mind would drift as she wondered about the boy's initiation and her friend Toyuk. But with so many girls living together and so many things to learn each day, she didn't have much time to think.

Ona was asked to come to the girl's initiation hut and share basket weaving techniques and decorative clothing style applications. Ona even brought Shushe one morning to share with the girls some cooking tips but didn't feel very welcome because of the other elder women who didn't think much of Shushe and her low tribal status. Shushe shared what she had, and Nea was the only girl who remained behind to thank Shushe for sharing her prize recipe.

Nea asked Shushe, "Have you seen Toyuk? How do you think he is doing?"

"You are a good friend, Nea. I am sure Toyuk is doing well." Shushe fought hard not to let any water cloud her eyes or spill out. "You better go to the next meeting, Nea. The elder women are waiting for you."

"Bye, Shushe," Nea said with a wave of her hand as she skipped down the trail to the flock of girls following an elder woman by the river while Shushe slipped quietly back to the main camp area unnoticed by anyone.

The girls were being shown the clothing washing area and some special techniques. This led to a lot of eye rolling and sighing, for the girls had already been washing clothes for many years. After the lecture the girls were given a little free time while the chosen girl and three of her friends were preparing lunch for all of the girls and elder women. Most of the girls began to wade out into the shallow part of the river. Soon many were swimming, splashing, and playing.

The tranquil scene was quickly made serious with the sight of a mountain lion. One girl screamed which brought men running. Girls were dashing out of the water and the camp went on alert. The mountain lion turned and retreated after hearing men shouting and slipped back into the woods and up the side of the ridge. Everyone was gathering together when one girl asked where Nea was. The search began and girls and elder women began looking for her and calling her name.

One girl down by the river shouted, "I think I see her!"

The girl could see long black hair floating in the water tangled up in a tree stump in the water by the bank in a particularly swift section. Nea was face down in the water and not moving. An elder woman told one of the girls to fetch the Chief and to send a man to fetch Tregor.

The first man to get to Nea gently turned her over in the water and she coughed, which made everyone relieved. When she was pulled from the water, her left leg below the knee was obviously broken. Her leg was swollen and she was in great pain. She was taken to the girls' hut and the Shaman was called. Tregor came running into the area asking for Nea. Their lives would soon be changed forever.

A girl's status and marrying potential could change drastically if she was sickly, injured, or deformed in some way. Tregor thought to himself, "Kinar may not want Nea if she couldn't walk right."

The final trial had come. All of the boys had heard many stories about "The Hunt": a time where a boy becomes a man by surviving three days and nights alone with a mission to bring back a kill. A deer was highly prized as a kill. But the legendary story of the tribe was of Growlon and how he came back with his first large humpback bear kill on his final third day. Most boys come back with a raccoon or a rabbit, but all wanted a buck with a full set of antlers. Even a doe was better than a smaller animal.

The morning was greeted again with silence in the boys' camp. Even though all of nature sang loudly this morning, the boys were sluggish. No one was very happy; none of the boys had eaten in three days. They were instructed to be ready for the Hunt. The boys began to pack up their needed items for the next three days. Their newly fashioned weapons were the only ones allowed except for a knife and a tool pouch, which carried a flint and tinder.

The elders gathered the boys together and gave them their final instructions.

"Your vow of silence ends now, but do not speak to each other for the next three days. You may ask an elder any question you may have, but do it alone. You may now eat anything you can provide for yourself. You cannot share food with another. You may not hunt together. If you see another tracking a prey, you may not share in the hunt or hunt the prey even if the other is not successful. You are not to camp together. You may not camp within the line of sight of another. Come back on the third day before sundown with the skin or animal part of what you were able to kill. If you do not come back by the fourth day we will send others to look for you, so be sure to come back on the third day. If you were successful on the first day, you may return anytime on the third day. On the evening of the third day at the tribal camp homecoming celebration you will finally know whether you passed your manhood initiation and will become a full tribe member. Now go, may the spirits be with you and give you favor."

Toyuk set out immediately sprinting for his favorite fishing hole. He thought only to get a full stomach before making any other decisions. Fresh berries gathered in a pile and several large rainbow trout roasting over the fire Toyuk had built did not take long to eat. Trout never tasted so satisfying to Toyuk. It felt so good to have a full stomach. He laid down after his meal on a large rock and let the sun soak into every pore of his body. He awoke with a start. The sun shone straight overhead.

"Time to get tracking," Toyuk thought to himself. He jumped off the rock, gathered up his weapons, and headed east higher up into the mountain range. As he climbed the ridge out of the valley he took one last look at the wisps of smoke coming from his tribal camp down in the valley next to the river.

As he hiked he became acutely aware of his surroundings. Sounds, wind direction, and his own breathing became his focus. He was a silent hunter completely aware and dangerous. He remembered a story Miccoon told of a hunting party who had been successful in a hunt for deer over the ridge next to the twin lakes, and he decided to head in that direction. Toyuk wanted to return on the third day with the antlers from a large buck.

He remembered the stories told by the Shaman around the communal evening fires about the spirit of the deer and their guardian. The guardian of the deer was a great white buck which ruled over all of the deer. He would allow men onto his sacred ground and had the power to bless or curse the hunter. Many hunters prayed to the great white buck for a blessing so that their hunts would be successful. No one had ever seen a white buck, and Toyuk wondered if the Shaman saw the animal after chewing some of that stuff in the sweat lodge. He felt himself getting angry.

"I will only pray to the Great Spirit," Toyuk found himself saying out loud. He stopped and took note of his surroundings. He listened and stopped breathing to listen completely. His eyes scanned in every direction. *"It isn't smart to hunt with emotions; they make one less focused."* His thoughts turned to all of the advice Miccoon had given him; he could almost hear him in his head giving him instructions. After calming himself, he continued his progress toward the twin lakes. He knew that the deer were sometimes found around the smaller of the two lakes where fresh grass was growing on the banks. This meant that Toyuk would have to circle around and come over the ridge from the other direction so that the wind would not give away his scent. It meant hiking the long way around, and Toyuk thought he might find a good place to sleep and spend the night if he came from the other direction.

Tomorrow I will see if there are any deer in the area and where I need to place myself for the best chances of a kill. But first I need supper. Toyuk was running through his mind what he needed to do when a jackrabbit raced across his path.

"Thank you, Great Spirit, for supper," Toyuk spoke out loud as he unpacked his bow, notched an arrow in place, and set off after the jackrabbit. That evening's fire made roasted rabbit. Toyuk had broken an arrow when he missed with his first shot and hit a rock. But the second arrow found its target. He sat by the fire whittling several more arrows with his father's knife.

Toyuk thought to himself, *"When I take another shot I cannot miss. I may not get a second chance if the deer get spooked and take off."* Toyuk used the meditation method to go over in his mind what he had done wrong in hunting the jackrabbit; he was determined not to make a mistake with a deer. Toyuk had made camp under the overhang of a huge rock boulder. His sleep was peaceful and deep until the early morning when his recurring dream returned. He awoke thinking about the conversation with Ona. In the morning Toyuk had a rabbit's foot hanging from his tunic and a rabbit fur tucked around his pouch. He was feeling good and was ready to scout out the lakes.

The feeling of the tribe was gloomy; Nea's accident left everyone feeling sad. Nea had such potential, but now with a leg that looked like she would forever be deformed, her marital prospects were gone—at least any prospect that held any kind of status.

Tregor was devastated. He disappeared from camp every morning and returned late after the sun had already gone down. His tender care for Nea was obvious and the Shaman had given advice that didn't seem to sit well with Tregor. Nayee was Tregor's wife and Nea's mother. Nayee worked hard at following all of the Shaman's medicinal instructions for Nea's condition. Nea's younger brother and sister tried hard to help with doing all the chores Nea usually had to do. Many tribal members tried hard not to look at a very distraught Tregor and Nayee.

Tregor sometimes could be seen visiting the Shaman and after the meeting would storm off into the woods. The look on Tregor's face was one of pure anger and no one wanted to approach Tregor while he was in one of those moods.

Late in the evening, Tregor confided what the Shaman had been saying to him to Nayee. "He says I am to blame. I didn't do the right things to appease the spirits. He says that I angered the spirits and that they took it out on Nea. He says that I must now pay for him to find out what I did wrong, and then he will tell me what I need to do. He said it will cost us much. I have searched my heart and the only thing that comes to me is that I may have favored some boys over others, but I am uncertain how that would have angered the spirits. I think the Shaman may not have our best interests in his mind. I don't know what to do."

"We have to do what he says, Tregor. What else can we do?" Nayee replied as gently as possible in a whisper.

"I don't know. I don't...." Tregor's voice trailed off.

6

THE GREAT WHITE BUCK

The hike to the lakes seemed to be shorter than Toyuk had expected, or maybe it was because he was feeling so good. Toyuk slowly crept on his stomach to the edge of the rock face, which towered above the main lake to peer over. In between two bushes Toyuk scouted the twin lake area, and just as it had been said a small herd of deer was grazing on the grass around the smaller lake. Toyuk smiled to himself; he had found his prize. He saw one buck among the herd, not too old by the looks of his antlers, but he was still a buck. Toyuk began to look for a place to approach the shot, which he would take tomorrow after placing himself in a hidden area early in the morning before the sun rose.

After finding what he thought would be the ideal place to hide for the next day's hunt, Toyuk slowly slid backward away from the rock face, and began to head towards the stream which fed the twin lakes.

Time for fish and dinner, he thought to himself. Toyuk found a nice size pool in the stream, and it wasn't long before the cooking fire was roasting trout. After Toyuk had finished his dinner, he began going over all of his hunting tools: the bow, string, arrows, pouch, and his father's knife. He felt that he needed some better-quality arrows for the two arrowheads he was carrying in his pouch. The arrowheads had been a gift from Miccoon, and Toyuk didn't want to waste them on arrows that weren't straight enough for a long shot. He set out to carve the straightest arrows he could fashion for tomorrow's hunt. *"The shot of a lifetime,"* his mind kept saying, would happen tomorrow.

Toyuk wondered how Buldar was doing and where he was. He thought about Nea, but he quickly changed his thoughts to think of something else. He worked diligently to fashion the two arrows. Miccoon's training of feather placement had prepared Toyuk to craft two arrows. *Almost as good as I've ever seen*, Toyuk thought to himself. By this time the sun had set and Toyuk was noting the placement of the moon so as to know when he needed to get up to find his hiding place for the morning hunt.

Once the moon began to set, Toyuk got up and began his descent to his chosen hiding place to be ready for first light. As he walked his senses were on alert, the nighttime required one to move with determined stealth. When Toyuk descended down the ridge around the rock face, he began to see a strange glow coming from one of the larger rock openings. As he came closer to the crack, the glow intensified and became brighter. His curiosity and wonder guided him off his desired path to check out the brightening glow. He had to climb some of the granite to even get to a place to see in the crack. When his head crested a rock, his eyes were struck by white light coming from something Toyuk could not yet see. After his eyes adjusted to the light, Toyuk looked upon something he thought didn't exist—a great white buck with antlers bigger than he had ever seen before. The white buck was situated within a stone's throw and hemmed in on three sides and looking straight at Toyuk. The glow of white light was coming from the buck. Toyuk was frozen in the position he first saw the magnificent glowing animal.

Something in his head told him, *"Rise and kill!"* Toyuk fumbled with his bow and notched one of his newly created arrows. Amazingly the great white buck never moved and Toyuk had to move to get into position to fire his bow. As Toyuk steadied himself on the granite of the rock face, his foot gave way when some of the loose granite crumbled underneath him; he was now falling to the bottom of the large crack.

When Toyuk awoke the sun was straight overhead, the birds were singing, and he saw a hawk circling overhead. He was dizzy and lightheaded, and even the air seemed different somehow. His body ached as he rose, but he found that he had not broken any bones. He began searching for his bow and arrows. Things seemed different than what he thought had seen the night before, his head still felt fuzzy, and his gaze couldn't find anything of his bow or arrows.

If he couldn't find his arrows, and he desperately looked for his father's knife, but it was nowhere to be found, then what would he say to his mother, Miccoon, Buldar, and others? Would anyone believe him about the glowing great white buck? Could he return to the tribe with only a rabbit pelt? He quickly felt around his waist for the pelt, but it wasn't there. Now he didn't even have the rabbit pelt. Toyuk felt dizzy and sat down hard.

"What is going on, Great Spirit?" Toyuk found himself speaking out loud. Only the breeze could be heard. Toyuk instinctively looked up. Toyuk blinked and rubbed his eyes; he had never seen anything like it in the sky. He saw something so high he couldn't make it out, but it was drawing a straight white line high overhead. Toyuk watched the white line slowly stretch across the sky.

What are you trying to tell me, Great Spirit? More silence. *Maybe the Great Spirit wants me to follow the white line,* Toyuk thought to himself.

He got up slowly and began to climb the rock to get out of the large crack in the face. As he climbed over the rock and reached the other side, now even the forest seemed different. There were more trees; the forest had gotten denser somehow. Things didn't seem right; he even began to notice how many of the trees were dead. He had never seen so many dead trees. The question of why there were so many more trees and many standing dead ones was one of the many increasingly confusing questions in Toyuk's mind. This was not the forest Toyuk was used to living in. He began to wonder where he was, but some of the rock faces in the distance still reminded him that he was still in the same area. The trees and even the forest floor seemed drastically different. He began to realize that the line in the sky pointed in the direction of his tribe's valley.

Should I return to my tribe and be ashamed that I have no trophy, and thus be denied graduation and unable to take my place in the tribe? What would Miccoon think? How would his failure affect his mother? I wonder how Buldar did. What had happened to change the forest so drastically? Did the others also notice the difference? Was he dreaming now? Questions raced through his mind. A pinecone fell and bounced into Toyuk causing pain in his arm.

"Nope—I'm not dreaming," he said to himself out loud. The changes in the forest were now disturbing Toyuk greatly and he began to jog towards his valley. "No matter what happens, I will return to my village and tell my story just as it happened. Obviously things have changed, and the tribe will be able to explain them to me."

Toyuk just wanted to be home with each step he took. His jog began to be more of a run. Everything seemed to have happened so long ago, and he felt that he didn't even fit into this forest.

Later in the afternoon when Toyuk crested the ridge of his valley—he noticed that there was no smoke at all in the valley. *Where were the cooking fires? Was his tribe even there? Was his family and tribe gone?* Questions now caused his heart to beat even faster. The trail path down into the valley was now gone and Toyuk stumbled as he ran down the side of the ridge into the valley. Shrubs and trees always seemed to be in his way as he descended into the valley of his tribe.

As he got to the floor of the valley, the water in the river seemed especially low in comparison to the day before. The forest was so much thicker and dense on the floor of his valley. The oak trees seemed so much older and there were so many fallen logs and standing dead trees. By now Toyuk was almost sprinting to the area where his village was. When he got to the place where the village was supposed to be, it didn't exist. The clearing had tall trees growing in it. Toyuk ran to the communal grinding rock. The grinding holes looked old and deeper, some had been filled with dirt and pine needles, and the grinding rock looked like it hadn't been used in ages. He ran to the diving rock. The river had moved a long way from the rock, which he thought was the one he used to dive off. No living areas, no tribe, no family.

"What happened, Great Spirit?" Toyuk shouted at the heavens. The white line in the sky was gone.

7

DEBATE AND DECISION

Toyuk stood silently, slowly turning around in circles gazing at the area surrounding him. There was no doubt in his mind that this was where his tribal village used to be, but certainly had not been here for a long period of time. He tried to think of every possibility of what could have happened to the tribe but the growth and change of the area dismissed everything and situation he could come up with.

His thoughts then began to turn to the question of why his tribe had possibly moved from this location. He remembered some conversations between elders of their desire to move to the foothills next to the great valley so that they could begin growing corn and other foods. He remembered that there was much discussion about hunting versus growing crops. He thought of their Chief and how he had stated that their tribe was a hunting tribe, and he was not one who wanted to always be digging in the dirt.

"Men hunt. Women tend crops and cook." Toyuk remembered the Chief's words distinctly. But he still wondered if the tribe had moved to the foothills. He had been to the foothills only once in his life and that was when he was small, but he remembered it to be a very long walk and a many day hike. But without the tribe where he was now standing, he could think of no other course of action.

His stomach growled.

I need to eat, he thought to himself. Toyuk promptly headed towards the river to fish. His regular fishing holes had changed and there seemed to be a lot less fish. Toyuk was able to catch one large fish but not any more. He had difficulty getting the fire started since his pouch seemed to be missing the flint and he had to use the long method of rubbing sticks together. The one fish did satisfy but he wondered what he would do on his trek to the foothills. He thought of trying to make a new bow and arrows but without his father's knife or his old sharp knife it would be impossible to fashion the thin arrows.

"I'll have to use throwing spears; I can still make those." Toyuk was now talking to himself out loud.

The rest of the day Toyuk searched and worked making one usable throwing spear, rubbing the tip of the branch against the rocks. There were no signs of any shelters anywhere and the changes in his surroundings, the river, the forest, the lack of fish, no village, made Toyuk very uneasy. He made a pine needle bed—there seemed to be more pine needles than he'd ever seen—then threw on a large dead log on the fire and tried to sleep.

Toyuk's dream had returned, except this time there appeared a being like a man in shining white clothes. The being spoke to Toyuk in his language and not in the language of the people in the dream.

"You are now here. You must go to the foothills and into the great valley. Remember that the Great Spirit is always with you and has prepared you for this time."

Toyuk awoke with a start and sat up drenched in sweat. Never had the dream seemed so real. The being in white clothes had delivered a message to him—*it must be from the Great Spirit*, pondered Toyuk.

Toyuk lay back down and stared up at the sky. He saw something he had never seen before, a very small light slowly moving among the stars in the direction of the great valley. Could this be another sign guiding him in the direction he should go? He decided to get up and begin his journey to the great valley as the being dressed in white had instructed him to do. Toyuk gathered up his throwing spear and began his trek.

Walking wasn't hard with the moon shining brightly overhead. Even the moon now didn't look as white, but there was still plenty of light for making his way through the forest and out of the valley where his tribe used to live. The trails Toyuk were used to weren't there anymore but he still knew the general direction fairly well. He estimated that it was still in the middle of the night when he began walking and the sunrise was still a long way off. After the second ridge Toyuk began to not recognize the area and was venturing into a place where he began to check his bearings fairly often to make sure he was going in the right direction.

After coming down a particularly steep ridge he came upon it. From there it spread out in front of him, a rock path so smooth and flat he had never experienced anything like it. And down the center of the path ran a line like the color of the sun although not as bright. Toyuk felt the flat rock path, it was so smooth and warm and seemed to follow the ridge a long way.

Toyuk's ears picked up a sound he had never heard before. He strained to listen as he ran behind a rock for cover. The sound of a rushing wind was coming towards him. When he first saw it, he couldn't believe what his eyes were seeing: two stars flying just above the path at incredible pace much faster than anyone could run. The stars and sound quickly came closer and got louder, and Toyuk felt terrified of what might be next. But the stars just flew by on the rock path. When Toyuk looked over the rock, the stars now showed red embers flying just above the path which then disappeared around a tree out of sight, and the decreasing sound of the wind also soon went silent.

"Great Spirit, what was that?" Toyuk found himself speaking out loud.

A still small thought came to his head, *"Follow the path down the mountain, but do not walk on it, and stay out of sight from the path."*

Toyuk sat and was quiet for a time. *I don't understand this place. But what other choice do I have?* His thoughts went back to two days before when everything and every decision seemed so simple. Where could he be? And where could his tribe have gone? And where was he now? He decided to do as the small voice in his head had told him to do, follow the rock path—out of sight.

After several hours following the rock path, the light of pre-dawn began to brighten the night sky. Toyuk had now walked several miles following the path and keeping it in sight and himself out of sight wasn't exactly easy. No other stars had come, and the path seemed to go on forever, never changing its size as it curved and meandered down the mountainsides.

Daybreak was now upon him and he began to see things he had never seen before. Large shelters besides the rock path, some with light coming out of them. Toyuk figured if the voice had told him to stay out of sight from the rock path, he had better stay out of sight from the shelters as well. That meant Toyuk would have to venture quite a way around the shelters, which seemed to become more numerous as he went farther down the mountain. The sun had crested the mountain range and was now shining down on the mountains, foothills, and great valley. Every once in a while Toyuk caught a glimpse of the valley which he thought must be filled with people because the air seemed so dirty from all of the cooking fires.

From a distance up the hillside, he could see the rock path. It followed every curve of the mountain as it slowly descended. Then Toyuk stopped and stared hard at the rock path; something was coming up the path. He dropped behind a bush and watched. Something almost as large as one of their shelters was slowly moving up the path. It didn't look like an animal or anything he had ever seen. As it got closer, Toyuk thought he saw people inside the shelter as it moved up the rock path. He could now hear the thing and it sounded like the stars from the night but not quite; this sound was lower and louder. Now he knew why he should not be walking the rock path—he wouldn't know how to deal with one of those large *things*.

I've never heard any story that could explain those things, thought Toyuk to himself. Many things were so different that Toyuk knew he was no longer in the same place, but where and how he didn't have any ideas that he could even think of to explain these changes he was seeing, hearing, and experiencing.

He pondered if the Great Spirit might have taken the form of the white glowing buck and was now punishing him for trying to shoot the buck. *But didn't the voice tell him to rise and kill?* The debate went on in Toyuk's head, trying to figure out what had happened to him. There had to be a connection between the white stag, the Great Spirit, his dreams, and now the place he was experiencing. The pieces were now being worked on in Toyuk's brain, but the connections still escaped him.

The trek down the mountain was exhausting since it had been a while since Toyuk had eaten and had water. A barrier like one of their reed fences stood a small distance ahead of him, except this barrier was straighter and taller than he had ever seen. Toyuk figured that if he ran and jumped, he could get a third from the top. He ran, jumped, and hung on. *The barrier was surprisingly strong,* Toyuk thought. He began to climb, but as he went over the top he grabbed onto something and felt a pain he had never experienced before. This pain shot through his entire body and was coursing through him. The light began to go dark. He felt very sluggish, and he was falling. Toyuk never felt hitting the ground.

8

LIFE IS BUSY

"You're a dweeb, dork; you're so out of it." The verbal jab was stated loud enough for everyone to hear.

Most of the girls just snickered, pointed, and whispered to each other. Bethany was so tired of being made the target of the in-crowd, the cool girls. Bethany knew her parents would never let her wear what it would take to even begin to be accepted into the "cool" group. She just sighed and walked away.

Just then she spotted her older brother Michael heading down the sidewalk towards home. It was one of the very few times he wasn't in a sports practice. Bethany ran to catch up with him, relieved to finally leave school behind her for the day. She hated being a freshman in high school. Just a few more days and summer would be here, and she would be officially a sophomore. Michael had no problem with the social scene at school; he was well liked across many different social cliques. He was smart, good looking, and after the last year had grown six inches in height, making him taller than ninety-nine percent of all the girls at school. Michael was still fairly skinny, but he was also very athletic. He had no problem fitting in, his life was looking up, and next year he would be at the top of the game as a senior.

"Hey Michael! Wait up!"

Michael didn't turn but kept walking.

"At least next year I won't be a freshman," Bethany spoke as she caught up with her brother.

"Yeah, but you will still be an underclassman."

"Oh, you are soooooooo encouraging."

"Don't worry, sis. Every year it gets a little easier and a little harder."

"Thank you, oh wise one, and may I walk and not trip over the shadow of your increasingly big head."

"Hey, I could teach you a few things if you had an ability to listen."

"What and, like, let you drone on and on how great you are?"

"Anybody want a ride home?" a lady called from a SUV behind them.

"Mom, what are you doing going home so early?" Bethany said, truly surprised at seeing her mom.

Stephanie Peterson was a second-grade elementary teacher, and usually worked past five p.m. in her classroom before starting for home.

"I decided to knock off early and surprise you guys. How would you like a pizza and a family movie night?"

"Yeah!" Bethany shouted and she ran to get in the SUV.

Michael walked casually over to the SUV. As he climbed into the passenger seat, he said, "I was going to Riverpark to meet the group and we were going to catch a movie."

"The group" was his friends from school made up of about twenty teenagers. They often hung out together, studied together, and went to parties together.

"Alright, but you've got to be home by midnight. What time were you going to meet them?" asked Stephanie.

"Around six." answered Michael.

"What are you going to do for dinner?" Stephanie kept up the questions.

"Catch it at the Riverpark. Manvir is picking me up around 5:45; he said we could go to In & Out, and then to the gathering place around the dead fountain when friends start to arrive. Can I have 20 bucks?" Michael asked with pleading eyes and a smile.

"Sounds like fun. But ask your dad for the money. Bethany, let's stop at the market and pick up a movie you want to see." Stephanie was turning left into the shopping center.

"Mom, can I get two?" Bethany asked.

"Which two?" Stephanie said while parking the SUV.

"I'll show you, come with me." Bethany said as she bounced out of the SUV.

While Bethany and her mom got out of the van and headed into the store, Michael slipped into his headphones and sunglasses and put his head back thinking of ways to convince his dad out of 20 dollars. Hopefully his dad would get home before Manvir showed up.

It was a fairly typical Friday afternoon for the Peterson family. Life was extremely busy and fast-paced, and like everyone else there was little time given to any contemplation. Family togetherness had to be fought for because every sliver of time of everyone's schedule seemed to be spoken for. It's what it is like in the 21st century. But Erik and Stephanie Peterson had fought hard to maintain as much family togetherness they could get. But now that the kids were getting older, finding those times of togetherness was getting harder.

"Paging Chaplain Peterson, paging Chaplain Peterson. Please come to nurse station 3," the hospital intercom system sounded. Erik was spending this Friday afternoon at the local hospital as one of the volunteer chaplains. He regularly volunteered about 10 hours a week at the hospital helping with the patients who requested a chaplain or patients who were designated Christian on their admittance form. The hospital also knew of Erik's heart for children and often called him in situations where children were badly injured to help calm the patient.

"Chaplain Peterson, could you please report to urgent care?" The nurse was speaking very quickly. "They've got a kid who was revived after he was picked up by the big cat farm in the foothills; seems he grabbed the electrical fence wire and was knocked out. They've got him sedated because he was very disoriented and screaming in some funny language, he should be coming out of it soon and they would like you to be there and make sure the kid doesn't freak out again."

Erik turned and walked quickly to the elevator which led him to the ER on the first floor.

Toyuk was dreaming again—his nightmare dream! Or was he? He couldn't tell, but this seemed so real. The high flat place with his hands tied down tight. The people were speaking a different language, the strange lights, sounds, colors. He had things on his arms attached to a kind of a tree that had things hanging with ... it was all beyond his ability to put it into words. And he couldn't wake himself up, like he was able to do before when he was in his dream. This nightmare wasn't going to let him escape.

Chaplain Peterson walked into the ER wing and approached the nurse's station. A nurse just pointed to a bed. Erik turned and saw a smallish boy, he guessed maybe 12 years of age from his size. The boy's eyes were wide and darting about the room. Erik thought he looked Native, but he wasn't sure. The boy was extremely dirty, his hair was longer, and his hands and feet were much more weathered than they should be. Erik wondered if this boy had ever worn shoes.

Toyuk saw a man approach slowly towards him. He heard the man speak to him in a language he didn't know, but his voice was calm.

"Son, are you okay?"

Toyuk's eyes narrowed.

"Where are you from?" Erik placed his hand on the boy's arm.

Toyuk let out a warrior's yell. "Kaaaaaaaaaayeeeeeeee!" Everyone in the ER turned and looked and then went about their business.

"Settle down, son, no one's going to hurt you here. We're here to help you." Erik tried to use his calmest voice possible in lowered tones, keeping his hand on the boy's arm.

Toyuk looked at the man's face. He didn't seem to be a threat. He was talking in a strange language calmly. Then the man just turned and walked away.

"Nurse, what's the complete story with this boy?"

"I don't know a thing, Chaplain. We were hoping you could decipher or get something out of him. All he does is the strange yell." The nurse looked perturbed and handed Erik the boy's file. "Ever since he became conscious, we've learned he doesn't speak English, and it's like he just appeared out in the woods from nowhere. It's almost like those stories of those kids found living all alone in the wilderness, and they're wild as an animal. But this kid at least had on something that looked like ancient Native garb. He's certainly a mystery to us, we were hoping you could help in some way."

"Has a translator been called yet?"

"No. We're not sure if he speaks any language or what nationality he is. All we've heard is his yell."

"He looks Native to me." Erik looked at the nurse hoping for more.

"Well, Chaplain, he's your case now." The nurse turned and directed her attention elsewhere.

Erik went back to the bed with the boy. In his calmest voice he spoke to the boy, "I'm going to see if I can find someone who can speak your language, I'll be back, don't worry." Erik smiled and patted the boy's shoulder.

Toyuk saw the man walk towards him. He was speaking the strange language again, and now touching his shoulder. Toyuk narrowed his eyes as the man spoke, but then the man smiled. *What did this man want with him? And why couldn't he wake up from this nightmare?* Then the man walked away. Toyuk was so tired. Now one of the women approached him and adjusted one of the things on the skinny tree, and he began to feel sleepy again.

"We'll keep him sedated so he doesn't hurt himself," the nurse spoke to Erik as he walked by the nurse's station.

"I'm going to see if I can find a translator."

"Well, bring him tomorrow. This boy is going to be asleep for a while."

When Erik got home and the family had finished dinner and the kids retreated to their rooms, Erik discussed his new case with wife.

"I've never seen anything like him, Steph. It's like one of those stories you hear about children who were raised by animals in the wilderness, except this boy was wearing some kind of clothing—but nothing like we know, it almost seems like an ancient costume—but less, I don't know. He certainly isn't from around here."

"How old would you say he is?" Stephanie asked.

"He looks about 12 but small for his age—even though his hands and feet look really weathered, like he's never worn shoes before, and like he's done hard labor." Erik shook his head. "I'm hoping that the court appointed translator can help tomorrow. I'd really like to know if the kid can communicate."

"What, Dad? You've found the Encino Man, like from the movie? Or maybe he's a relative of Mowgli the jungle boy?" Bethany had entered the living room and had heard her father's last remarks.

"Funny, Bethany, funny," Erik said deadpanned as Bethany entered the kitchen and came out with a glass of milk. "This kid needs our help, and I just hope I can find a way to reach him."

"You'll help him, Dad. You always help those kids from the hospital. Just don't bring him home like the last one."

"Hey, it was only for one night until foster care got their act together."

"Sure, Dad, sure," came the response from down the hallway. "Hey, mom, let me know when movie night begins."

"Okay, honey," Stephanie yelled in response.

"It's like we really never see them anymore, with all their homework, and them on their phones and computer," Erik said with a dejected tone in his voice.

Stephanie replied with a hopeful tone, "Yep. So maybe we can get them to watch a movie with us tonight. I got one Beth wanted to see—I'm just not sure Michael will want to join us."

"Yeah, he's seen most everything before we ever see a movie. If he hasn't seen it with his friends, he's seen it on his computer. Computers have stolen our family movie night from us."

"Let's hope for the best," Stephanie said as she got up from the couch and headed for the kitchen. "Hey, Hun, you want some cookies and ice cream for the movie?" she called from the kitchen.

"Sure. Just one scoop though," Erik called back as he headed to put in the disk.

I wonder why I want to watch the classics like Tarzan and Jurassic Park now, thought Erik. Hmmm... research.

9

THREE YEARS LATER

"Toyuk — would you please help me unload the groceries?"

"Yes, Mrs. Peterson," Toyuk said in English, which seemed to be getting better day by day even though he always seemed to have an accent and was unable to say certain words correctly. Toyuk jogged out to the SUV to help Stephanie with the bags of groceries.

Toyuk had been taken in by Erik and Stephanie as a foster child and quickly became one of their family, learning quickly from the Peterson children about life in their home and city. Toyuk was home-schooled now by Stephanie after she lost her job at the school district because of staffing cuts. She did tutor on the side and had joined a city network of many other homeschooling families in the area. Both Erik and Stephanie had talked about adopting Toyuk and were going through the legal process but hadn't told Toyuk or their own kids of their plans. They knew Michael and Bethany would be for it since they continually brought up the subject to their parents.

In three years Toyuk had grown and grown and grown. He was now about five feet, eleven inches and a very muscled 175 pounds since he had begun to work out with Michael in the family's gym in the garage. He was constantly learning about this new world the Great Spirit had thrust him into. He was continually marveled by the technology of this world. Cell phones, huge flat screen TVs, cars, planes, kitchen appliances, washing machines. And the video games—oh, how he excelled at the first-person shooter/adventure games. So many areas of new things swam in his head every day with so many questions and so many things to read.

The Petersons took Toyuk to their church on Sundays. Toyuk usually sat and keenly observed closely the people in the church. He answered when questioned but with very few words. He was often described as a quiet one by others, but the Peterson family knew the real Toyuk: a deep thinker with a philosopher's heart, a teen with a well-reasoned and quick mind who had very strategic questions. He often could size up a person within hearing a few words from the speaker. He was extremely adept at reading people's body language—at least that's what Stephanie constantly told him.

Toyuk's dreams had stopped. He was now living in the dream. He didn't know how he had come to this world and had no clue if or when he would or could ever get back to his previous life. The church experience left him with many questions of which he pondered and wondered if the Great Spirit would answer all of his ponderings. But the Great Spirit had been silent for the time he was now living in. He inherently knew that the traditions of the Peterson tribe and their church were much the same as his own tribe back home. It was a community with its own traditions and rituals. They were vastly different and the same in many ways. The pastor ("Shaman" in Toyuk's mind) took his place before the congregation (tribe) and taught the stories of the book (stories of the spirits) just like Toyuk saw his own tribe's Shaman teach his followers, although this pastor didn't seem as devious or theatrical as his own Shaman. Toyuk observed carefully. He observed that the Peterson family held fairly high status within the congregation the way people came to greet them.

"Helloooo, Toyuk!" Erik was trying to get Toyuk's attention, but Toyuk was in one of his "thinking" modes and seemed oblivious to anyone around him. "Toyuk," Erik spoke now with a much more direct volume.

Toyuk now heard Mr. Peterson and turned to look at him.

"We've got to go. Get in the car."

Toyuk jogged over to the car and jumped in. They were headed to the hospital as he agreed to go with Mr. Peterson as he did his rounds as a Chaplain. The sights and sounds made him think of his own waking moments in that hospital which seemed so long ago.

Life in the new world was becoming normal for Toyuk until ...

On nights Toyuk couldn't sleep he would head out of the house to the horse barn and commune with the horses and animals. He found the horses to be magnificent animals and wondered what his tribe would do with such an incredible alliance with such animals. Toyuk had learned to ride as Bethany had taught him many horse-riding skills and ways with the family's farm animals. He felt he could relate to the animals almost better than with these people of this world.

It was then during one such night that Toyuk saw Him outside the barn door, just past the fence. The White Buck stood still looking directly at Toyuk. The Great Spirit spoke in Toyuk's mind, *"You must learn of Me. Learn My story."*

Then the White buck just disappeared. It didn't run away; it just faded from Toyuk's sight like a ... ghost.

Toyuk was jolted in his mind and heart. Memories flooded his mind of his own past. The trials, his mom, Miccoon and Ona, Buldar, and then ... Nea. What had become of them? What did they do when he didn't return from the hunting trial and manhood rituals? His heart sank. He felt bad for not thinking of them more.

"Great Spirit... teach me your ways. Teach me your Story," Toyuk whispered in the dark of the barn.

As he turned to go through the barn back to the house and his bedroom, his mind was spinning from this latest encounter with the Great Spirit. He was wondering if he should tell Erik and Stephanie about it when he was immediately blinded by a light so bright coming from the loft in the barn that he fell backwards into a stall.

"Toyuk. Why are you so sad?!" a booming Voice asked.

Toyuk couldn't look towards the voice, he just kept his head down because the light was just too bright.

"Who ... are ... you? Are you the Great Spirit?" Toyuk's voice quivered as he tried to speak. He could feel a frequency vibration beginning to go through his body like an electrical current.

"I am HIS Son," the Voice spoke with warmth and love. The Voice had a different quality to it. To Toyuk it seemed that the Voice was that of many running waters, deep, rich, and powerful.

Toyuk immediately put his face flat into the straw. He had never encountered anything so powerful.

"You can learn about me in a book called the Bible. In that book I am named Jesus. Read about me. Learn my story. But first you will need my Holy Spirit to guide you and teach you. He must fill you and indwell you. You must allow Him to possess you completely. He has been speaking to you even when you were back in your own world."

"Jesus?" Toyuk whispered.

"Yes, my friend?" The Voice was filled with love.

Toyuk raised his head and looked at the glowing figure sitting on the edge of the barn loft. He could stand the light somewhat better, although it still seemed a little painful to look at. There sat this Jesus with a huge smile on his face, looking directly at Toyuk.

"Help me," was all Toyuk could get out of his mouth even though his mind was swimming with thoughts, questions, memories, and emotions all raging at light speed in his heart and head.

"I will." Jesus said with firm conviction and love.

Toyuk then heard Jesus begin to blow from his mouth. Toyuk felt immediately a shiver go through his entire body. Powerful, warm waves of vibration and love began to wash right through him. The waves of power and love from the breath of the Glowing One were almost too much to take, when Toyuk lost consciousness.

Toyuk awoke the next morning in the barn to the rooster crowing.

"Was that a dream? Did last night really take place?" Toyuk wondered in his mind.

"*YES, I AM REAL!*" came a booming Voice in the mind of Toyuk. "*And I will remain with you as LONG as you want me to. I will teach you My ways.*" The Voice was quick in response to Toyuk's mind's questions.

"Don't EVER leave me!" Toyuk shouted out loud, he startled himself in the loudness of his own voice.

"I will never leave you. I will always be here when you need Me." The Voice in Toyuk's head sounded a lot like the glowing Son Jesus' voice last night but a little different.

Toyuk headed back to the house with a determined resolve to learn about this Jesus. He also wondered about the speed at which his own questions were answered by this Spirit Jesus, this Son of the Great Spirit. He also wondered about this "Holy Spirit'" Jesus had talked about and who He was.

"So much to learn," Toyuk thought to himself.

Toyuk burst through the house looking for the book Jesus had talked about. His movements and noises had Stephanie coming out of the master bedroom to see what all the noise was.

"You're up early. What are you doing?" Stephanie said with somewhat of an exasperated tone.

"I'm looking for a book," Toyuk said as he continued to rummage through the shelves.

"Which book?" Now Stephanie was fully exasperated.

"Uh, a babla maybe? How did He say it again?" Toyuk was still focused on finding the book and not looking at Stephanie.

"Who? What? You're not making any sense, Toyuk. What is going on with you?" Stephanie was now standing with a hand on her hip.

"Jesus, what was the name of the book again?" Toyuk's mind threw the question out.

"Bible," came back from the Voice in Toyuk's head.

"I'm looking for a ... Bible," Toyuk turned and said to Stephanie Peterson.

"ERIK! Get in here!!" Stephanie shouted towards the bedroom.

Erik stumbled out of the bedroom as Toyuk continued to look for a Bible amongst the bookshelves.

"What's going on? What's the problem?" Erik was looking at Stephanie and then to Toyuk watching him scour the bookshelves.

"The boy has lost it!" Stephanie said to Erik.

"What's going on? What are you looking for, Toyuk?" Erik was now walking towards Toyuk.

"A Bible," both Stephanie and Toyuk said at the same time.

"Wait ... stop... Toyuk. I'll get you a Bible." Erik turned and headed towards his home office. Toyuk and Stephanie followed.

"What happened, Toyuk? Why the sudden interest in the Bible at this time in the morning?" Erik looked at Toyuk and wondered which version and translation to give to Toyuk from the many Bibles on his bookshelf. "Wait, don't you have and use a Bible in your homeschooling?" Erik asked.

"Yes, but it's The Good News version, Erik," Stephanie said.

"*Wait—you are ... that ... Jesus?*" Toyuk spoke in his mind towards heaven.

"*Yes.*" The Voice was laughing in Toyuk's mind.

Toyuk's mind was spinning. Gears were grinding while others were being put into place.

"*Do I tell them Jesus?*" Toyuk wondered how much of the story he should tell them. They really never were able to get all of Toyuk's history and past story out of him. He held that information very close to himself. He would only answer as succinctly as possible when questioned about his past. Now with this latest encounter, Toyuk was scared no one would ever believe him about any of it.

"*Tell them. But you must understand it will take them a while to believe you.*" The Voice was gentle and loving in its tone and inflection in Toyuk's mind.

"What is going on, Toyuk? Why the sudden interest?" Erik was calmer now and sitting at his desk.

"The Son of the Great Spirit says I can tell you—but that you may not believe me right away."

Both Erik and Stephanie had never heard Toyuk speak that way. Stephanie went to sit on the love seat in the office. Both of them remained silent and looked intently at Toyuk, waiting for him to continue.

Toyuk began his story talking about his tribe's valley high in the mountains. He told them about his mother, Miccoon and Ona, his father's story, or at least the part he knew about it, and the manhood trials and his friends. Then Toyuk paused for strength and felt a comforting Presence in his chest. The Voice in his mind said, "*Go ahead — I'm with you, tell them.*" So Toyuk began to tell them of the dreams he had and the White Buck experiences back in his world. He told them about the Shaman and the teachings of the spirits. Toyuk allowed his past to spill out of him like a wide vista. He then recounted the cleft in the rock on the hunt, the White Buck, and suddenly being thrust into this world, although he didn't know where this world was. He recounted the trek down the mountain, trying to climb the fence, and waking up in the hospital. Both Erik and Stephanie were extremely silent as Toyuk talked more than they had ever heard him before. The Petersons' world was about to be rocked even further.

Toyuk continued his story and began to tell them of the last night's happenings. Toyuk recounted all the words the Son of the Great Spirit named Jesus told him and what being in His Presence was like. Then Toyuk shared that Jesus blew on him and he just went to sleep.

"Um ... thank you Toyuk for telling us your story," Erik said to Toyuk with hesitation in his voice. "I think your mom and I need to talk right now. We'll talk with you a little later."

"Could I have a Bible please?" Toyuk asked Erik.

Erik handed a leather-bound Bible to Toyuk, and Toyuk turned and walked out of the room. Toyuk continued out of the house and headed to the barn.

Erik and Stephanie looked at one another.

"Wow," said Erik.

"I don't know what to think," Stephanie replied.

"Do you think we need to have Toyuk speak to a counselor? He certainly believes what he said, but..." Stephanie was unsure what else to say. She didn't want to say the things that were running through her head, like they have a mental case living in their home or that Toyuk was the best liar she had ever encountered. "That can't be correct," she said to herself out loud.

"What do you mean that can't be correct?" Erik replied.

"I mean... I don't know what I mean... this is crazy." Stephanie was still reeling.

"Well, at least let's meet with Pastor Jim and have Toyuk tell his story to him and see what he says. What do you think, Steph?" Erik was looking for some kind of sense of understanding.

"Yeah I guess—it couldn't hurt. But let's not discuss this with others, I mean what would people think?" Stephanie was already imagining the gossip circle at church, the things that could really fly, and their reputations being trashed.

Toyuk was in the barn thoroughly enjoying reading the Bible. It all made so much sense to him now. He dove into the Gospel of Mark, then Matthew, then Luke, and John. He didn't stop, and by the afternoon he had finished the book of Acts. He was overjoyed and truly sad. All he could think of was being able to share all of this with his Native family and tribe, but would he ever get back to them? So many need to meet this Son of the Great Spirit named Jesus. Reading the Bible was so easy with this Holy Spirit highlighting, prompting, teaching, and explaining the ways of the Great Spirit and Father of all creation. Slowly Toyuk began to understand how much the Holy Spirit was helping him learn. The Holy Spirit's Voice in Toyuk's mind was so much like the Voice of Jesus but it was also slightly different. He was beginning to tell the difference between the Voices entering his mind. He already was beginning to discern between his own mind's thoughts and the Voices of Jesus and the Holy Spirit. But there also now was an awareness of another's voice.

Erik called the church office to set up an appointment with Pastor Jim. After being on hold for five minutes, the assistant said that the soonest appointment available was next week on Thursday from 10:30–11am. The soonest one after that was in 3 weeks. Erik took the Thursday appointment.

10

CONFRONTATION AND DREAMS

"So good to see you, Toyuk," Pastor Jim said as he shook Toyuk's hand vigorously. "Have a seat." Pastor Jim motioned to the family.

Erik, Stephanie, and Toyuk all took a seat on the large leather couch in Pastor Jim's big office. The office was beautiful with dark woods and leather furniture, a wall-to-wall bookcase filled with impressive-looking leather-bound books. The office, the desk, the furniture, all spoke to the impressive position of the person who occupied this office. Pastor Jim took a seat in a large high-backed leather chair next to the couch.

"Now how can I help you?" Pastor Jim said, smiling.

For an awkward moment there was a prolonged silence. Erik finally spoke up. "Pastor Jim, Toyuk has had a great interest in the Bible of late."

"Oh, that's very good!" Pastor Jim said somewhat enthusiastically.

Erik continued. "It comes from an encounter Toyuk had in our barn. I want Toyuk to explain."

"Go ahead son." Pastor Jim was trying to sound fatherly.

"The Great Spirit...." Toyuk paused to pray in his mind to the Great Spirit. *"What would you have me tell them?"*

"Just be honest with them," came the response to his mind.

"The Great Spirit has been giving me dreams since I was a boy." Toyuk continued to tell them most of his story, except for certain details he felt he needed to keep very private. He went on to share the complete encounter in the Petersons' barn with the Great Spirit's Son. After he finished Pastor Jim sat silently.

"Toyuk, would you mind if I talked with Erik and Stephanie privately for a moment? My secretary has some good cookies in her office."

Pastor Jim had gotten up and opened his office door and stretched out his arm. Toyuk got up silently and proceeded to walk out into the Pastor's secretary's office. Pastor Jim closed the door and sat back down in the big backed leather chair. Erik and Stephanie waited patiently to see what Pastor Jim would say.

"I know Toyuk has had a fairly traumatic time, especially from his hospital visit, and adjustment time with you folks over the last 3 years. Has he ever had any psychological testing done?"

"Yes. He went through all the battery of tests when we learned how to communicate with him," Erik spoke clearly and slowly. "He also has continued with some tests as he has had a better grasp of English. There have never been any indications that he has had any problems or anomalies, but it has taken some time to realize he was raised in a much different culture. We have yet to discover where exactly he came from."

"Well, from my training I can say I have only heard of something remotely like this from a few mentally challenged or emotionally disturbed patients Dr. Ameil has told me about. I think it might be good if Toyuk was tested again." Pastor Jim was speaking with an authoritative voice.

Stephanie quickly spoke up. "Toyuk has never displayed any mentally weird things the entire time we've known him. And I've not known him to be overly emotional; in fact, to me it seems he keeps his emotions deep inside him and rarely shows any. It's just within the last week when he told us his story that we didn't know what to do. That's why we called you. What about the spiritual side of his story, Pastor?"

"Well, we definitely know that God no longer works that way with people," Pastor Jim said in a matter-of-fact tone. "We know that because we have the Bible now to guide us." Pastor Jim's voice was beginning to sound like a Sunday morning sermon.

Stephanie couldn't help the frown beginning to show on her face. She always didn't like when Pastor Jim began to speak on this issue. In fact, Stephanie did not agree. She often wondered if some of her own dreams had been God trying to communicate with her. Stephanie knew there was a spiritual side beyond the intellectual but hadn't learned how to understand it. Erik and she had had discussions about the dreams in her past, but since she never explored them;

it became just a weird part that wasn't talked about. Stephanie herself began to greatly doubt what it all meant. Yet... There were those stories from her grandmother. But there was the whole thing in the church about weird people who have dreams, and she had worked very hard at dismissing and denying her own dream encounters to herself. *I am a "good" Christian*, she thought to herself. This whole spiritual side was just too controversial.

"I think we can chalk this up to teenage struggles to cope. Just have him keep reading the Bible," Pastor Jim said with a fake toothy smile.

Erik knew quickly that they would not get any real help from Pastor Jim. Erik stood up and said, "Thank you so much for your time, Pastor. We'll certainly take what you said into serious consideration. We'll closely monitor the situation with Toyuk." He shook Pastor Jim's hand as Stephanie stood up before they headed out of the office.

When they were in the car on the ride home, Toyuk finally spoke. "What did the shaman say? I mean Pastor."

Erik had been thinking about how to tell Toyuk what the Pastor's position was. "Pastor Jim doesn't agree that God works that way."

"Doesn't agree God works what way?" Toyuk was clearly confused.

"That God meets people, I mean in person, by visions, or encounters, like the one you talk about."

"Oh."

Toyuk had decided not to talk much. He knew that the Pastor / Shaman didn't believe him. Everything about the man reminded him of the Shaman in his own village: power-hungry, controlling, and always wanting to lord over others. Toyuk had been listening to his sermons for 3 years and often wondered if the man actually believed what he was preaching. Toyuk's conclusions were that Pastor Jim did not. Yet there were others in the church who did have a spiritual side to them which he recognized, like he did in Ona. Toyuk wondered how to continue with the Petersons and how much to tell them from this point forward. He wanted to have some alone time to discuss this with the Great Spirit and His Son to get some instructions and help.

The Bible he had gotten from Erik confirmed over and over that God used dreams, visions, and personal encounters to interact with people as Toyuk read and read through it faster and faster. The first part of the Bible was filled with stories of God encountering people He called Prophets. Then there was Saul's encounter with the Great Spirit's Son on the road to Damascus in the book of Acts. Saul/Paul went on to explain more about another part/person of God called the Holy Spirit. Toyuk was learning quickly and he began to slowly understand the Voices of the distinct Person(s) of God in his own spirit and mind.

That night Stephanie had a wildly clear vivid dream.

In her dream, Erik and she were walking towards their barn. Light streamed from inside the barn. Stephanie noticed all the cars and trucks parked in their driveway, and there were even more parked next to the barn. As she got closer to the barn, she heard music and the voices of a crowd inside. As she entered, she was greeted with hugs from mostly people she didn't know. There were a few women in the distance she recognized but they were women she only knew in passing because they weren't very well known in the church and didn't interact much with others. The barn was lit up with lights. People were sitting on hay bales and standing in groups. Then she saw her husband greet all the people and welcome them. That's when she noticed a group begin to play their instruments louder and sing. They sang songs she hadn't heard before, but immediately she felt like crying. What was going on?! People were standing, kneeling, sitting with their hands in the air—joining in in worship. Some were singing in a language she didn't recognize. Then the dream ended abruptly.

When she woke, Stephanie noticed she was crying. She looked over at Erik who was sleeping soundly. She thought about waking Erik, but then with all they were dealing with Toyuk she didn't want to bring up more stress. She thought Erik wouldn't want to hear her silly little dream. She rolled over and tried to go back to sleep. Sleep was not coming. The images of the dream were so vivid and clearly still in her mind. Her emotions were swirling like a stormy ocean. Stephanie didn't know why she was still crying. She then began to pray.

"Lord, I don't know what this is all about, but I want to know. I want to know You better. Help me." Stephanie noticed her prayer was much less formal sounding than her normal way of praying.

"Heavenly Father, I don't want to offend you by my normal words. Please forgive me. In Jesus Name. Amen."

Somehow she didn't feel better after her last prayer. *What am I doing?* she thought to herself. Then she thought she needed to talk to Toyuk privately about her dream. Then she wondered where that thought came from.

I am a mess, Stephanie thought. *Morning can't come soon enough.*

Erik after his morning shower found Stephanie sitting still in her PJs in the family room with a cup of coffee looking out the window at the barn with a far-away look on her face.

"Good morning, Hun. You're up early."

Stephanie didn't respond. In fact, it seemed like she didn't even hear him.

"I gotta run, Hun. Busy day today. See you later."

Erik was running just a bit behind and knew he had to get to the hospital for his scheduled time of Chaplaincy, as the day's agenda was busy. He went back into the kitchen to grab some food, making sure he didn't spill on his shirt, and headed out to the garage with his briefcase in hand.

Stephanie was still sitting there after the kids had slammed the door as they went off to school. *I've got to get going,* thought Stephanie.

She took a shower, got dressed, and decided to head into town to do some grocery shopping. The entire time she couldn't shake the images from the dream from her mind. She felt somewhat like a zombie walking the isles of the supermarket.

While Stephanie was looking over the meat counter an older man with a white beard, cap, and glasses approached her.

"Excuse me, ma'am. I know this is a bit unusual, but the Lord wants me to give you a Word. Would you mind?"

Stephanie was definitely caught off guard as she looked up at the older gentleman. "Uh—okay, I guess." *He certainly doesn't have the feel of a weirdo.*

"The Lord wants you to know that the dream you had last night was from Him. It is about your future. The Lord wants you to know that He loves you very much and wants to spend more time with you." He paused to consider his next words. "Now this part is a little different than I've heard before mam. The Lord says He sent the boy to you and you are to believe him and that the Lord would soon be taking him back to his home."

Stephanie felt like a deer in the headlights.

"Does this make any sense to you?"

"Who are you?" Stephanie asked.

"I'm sorry, how rude of me. My name is Mark. I just moved to this area. The Lord told me that I had an assignment here in this city."

"Thank you, Mark. I need to be going." Stephanie quickly pushed her grocery cart away from that man. *Crap! Why am I beginning to cry again?* Stephanie had heard of people having this weird kind of encounter with mystical types of people who said that they were "spirit-filled" Christians—but she had never had any kind of encounter like that before with anyone . . . other than Toyuk.

Those two encounters of the dream and the old man with a "Word" left Stephanie spinning emotionally for the rest of the day. She threw herself into busyness—putting away the groceries, laundry, cleaning the bathrooms. She felt almost too scared to pray.

Would God actually do something else to me if I talked to Him again? I don't think I can handle any more!

Erik made his rounds at the hospital visiting and praying with patients in the morning. But his preoccupied mind couldn't stop replaying the events of the previous day.

Pastor Jim was too quick to dismiss Toyuk's story, Erik thought. *He didn't even give the smallest hint that it could possibly be real. I know God can work in different ways. But is this actually from God? What do I really believe?* Erik suddenly remembered conversations with Stephanie about dreams she had had. *Why am I thinking about her dreams?*

"Brother Peterson."

Erik was startled by the voice. He turned around and saw an older man with a white beard, a cap, and glasses.

"Brother, the Lord sent me to give you a Word. He wants you to know to clean out your barn; He wants you to begin to have meetings in it."

After that the man in the beard and cap promptly turned around and walked away, leaving Erik thinking, *That was really strange!*

Erik went to the nurse's station to see if they could tell him about the older man. None of the nurses knew anything about him. It was time for him to go home. Erik hurried to his truck. He had a weird feeling he couldn't shake. *What was that about God? Do you really care about the cleanliness of my barn? What kind of meetings? Is this really you?*

In the truck Erik prayed aloud, "Heavenly Father you are all knowing. Father help me to understand your will for me, for us. Was that man really from you? What is it you want me to do? In the precious name of Jesus. Amen."

As quickly as Erik had ended his prayer the thought came to his mind. *"Clean out the barn." Okay, that's just weird!* "What's up God?" Erik found himself saying it out loud in a frustrated tone.

As he walked into the house and in the kitchen, he saw Stephanie. Together they said at the same time,

"We need to talk."

"You first." Again together. Both Stephanie and Erik laughed and then hugged. It felt good to both of them.

"I'll go first," Erik said softly.

"Today, literally out of the blue, this guy comes up to me while I was almost finished with my rounds and says he has a 'Word' for me. Get that—not the usual way you begin a conversation with a stranger. Then he said what he said and just turned around and walked away. Weird, huh?"

"Well, what did he tell you?" Stephanie now was really interested.

"What did he look like?" Stephanie was now asking before Erik had a chance to speak. "What was he wearing?" The questions kept coming.

Erik closed his mouth and waited to see how long the list of questions would be. Erik was also kind of glad Stephanie was so interested in what he had to say. She was intensely focused on what he was saying.

"Well...?"

"I just wanted to wait until you were finished with your questions. First he said God wants me to clean out the barn."

Stephanie dropped the spatula she was holding; it clattered to the floor. Erik just kept going.

"Second, he said God wants us to have meetings in it. He was an older man with a white beard and wearing a gray jacket and had on a cap."

"Did he have glasses?" Stephanie asked.

"Yes. Why do you ask?" Erik cocked his head.

"Was his name Mark?" Stephanie asked with squinted eyes.

"Wait...What? I never got his name. He left too quickly for me to ask him anything." Erik replied.

"Honey, let's go into the family room, I think you need to sit down and listen to my day now." Stephanie quickly told Erik about her encounter with Mark in the supermarket.

"Whoa. That's incredible," was all Erik could say. His mind was spinning.

"You think that's weird? Now I think I need to tell you about the dream I had last night." After Stephanie told Erik her dream, both felt a strong Presence they had not experienced before, at least not in this way. Both felt God's love and laughter.

"Okay. I think God is definitely up to something here," Erik said, chuckling quietly.

"YOU THINK!" Stephanie almost shouted it.

"I'm not sure I want to share this with Pastor Jim right now," Erik said quietly in a hushed voice.

Stephanie laughed. "He'd suggest we both seek psychological counseling," Stephanie said with a smirk.

"We're not crazy. There are just too many coincidences for it to really be a coincidence," Erik said.

"I'm glad we agree." Stephanie was just realizing she had had a real dream from the Lord; it sent all sorts of warm feelings flowing through her. "What do you think we should do now?"

"I don't know. Honestly. This is not my normal way of dealing with God."

"I just had a dream that was from God!" Stephanie said quietly and firmly.

"Things sure have changed in this house since Toyuk shared with us his story. I think we need to ask him some more questions."

"Yep. From what Mark said I think we need to do that. I'm just not sure what he meant about Toyuk being taken back home." Stephanie was standing looking out the window at the barn.

"Is there any way we can find out more about this Mark?"

"I was thinking the same thing," Stephanie agreed.

"I have no clue as to how to start." Just then a clear thought popped into Erik's mind. *You should ask God about it.* "Maybe we should ask God about it?"

"Funny you say that. I just had the same thought pop into my head." Stephanie was still staring at the barn.

"Okay, this is really getting weird."

"I am beginning to like it," said Stephanie. "At least we are on the same page. I haven't felt this close to you in years. I was always afraid to tell you my weird dreams. I thought I was different somehow, maybe that I actually had mental issues."

"You are the least weird person I know, Hun. Other than being a woman, which of course I still don't understand," Erik teased, coming up behind Stephanie at the window and putting his arms around her.

"Mmmm." Stephanie leaned back into her husband and let the crack about her womanhood slide.

11

⸺ ◆ ⸺

DIVINE APPOINTMENT

The Central Valley nights weren't exactly cool. Toyuk usually slept without any sheet over him. In the predawn he was awakened by the Voice of the Great Spirit speaking very loudly in his head.

"Toyuk, go to the corner of Olive and Broadway at 7:12 this morning and look for a man with a white beard, cap, and glasses. Greet him and ask him for the message I have given to him for you."

Toyuk knew he'd want to get Michael to drive him to the Tower District for this morning's meeting. He wasn't sure how to give this information to Erik and Stephanie about his latest instructions from the Great Spirit, so he figured he'd tell them after he met with the man. Toyuk wasn't sure what Erik and Stephanie were thinking after the meeting with their pastor yesterday.

Around 6:30 Toyuk caught Michael coming through the kitchen after returning from his morning run.

"Hey Michael, can you give me a lift this morning to the Tower District? I've got a meeting I've got to be at." Toyuk hoped that Michael wouldn't ask too many questions and would be agreeable to help him.

"When do you need this ride?" Michael said as he headed towards his room.

"I need to be in the Tower District at the corner of Olive and Broadway at 7am."

"Got a morning coffee meeting in the Tower, eh? That's cool. Yeah, I can help you. Let me grab a quick shower and we'll be off. But you'll have to find a way back. I've got to meet Joe at 7:30."

"Thanks, Michael, that's great. I'll be ready to go when you are."

On the ride over to the Tower District, Michael didn't ask Toyuk any questions, and Toyuk was completely fine being silent for the entire ride. They arrived just before 7, and Toyuk jumped out of the car, thanked Michael for the ride, and closed the car door. Michael quickly drove down Broadway towards his own meeting.

Toyuk found a good spot to just hang back and watch all the corners, waiting for the man he was told about. At 7:12 a man fitting the description was walking west on Olive on the north side of the street. When Toyuk spotted him, he walked toward the man.

The man stopped and watched Toyuk walk towards him. As Toyuk stopped in front of him the man greeted Toyuk warmly.

"You must be my divine appointment this morning," he said with a laugh in his voice.

Toyuk responded with, "The Great Spirit sent me. He said you have a message to give me."

"Yes, I do. The Holy Spirit gave it to me in a dream last night." The man began to share. "You are not of this time. I really don't know what that means, but He said you'd understand. God, or the Great Spirit as you know Him, wanted to let you know that He created you to be loved by Him. And that His Son Jesus died for you so that you could understand how much He loves you and wants to be in a relationship with you. He is very pleased with the relationship you are building with Him and He's given you many dreams throughout your life to let you know that you are loved by Him." He paused for a moment. "And your time here is coming quickly to an end, and He will be sending you back to your people with His message about the work and sacrifice of His son Jesus for them. But He also said that your homecoming would not be easy for your people or you, and that you are to rely on the words and instructions He gives you, and to obey them quickly and completely." A look came over his face. "I saw your face in my dream, so I knew what you looked like. I'm not sure I can answer any questions, as I only understand some of this message."

Mark looked at Toyuk's face and could see that Toyuk understood the message, but he also saw surprise as he told him that he'd be returning to his people.

"Oh yeah, I forgot to tell you.... that you'll only be able to bring one thing back with you besides the clothes on your body, is your Bible. That wasn't part of the message, but that's what I saw you holding as you walked through the forest—and I just knew that you were only allowed that as you traveled back to your people. I hope this helps you." Mark smiled as he put his hand on Toyuk's shoulder.

Toyuk's eyes began to water as he thought about Shushe, Miccoon, Ona, Nea, and Buldar.

Mark asked Toyuk, "Can I pray with you?" as they stood in the middle of the sidewalk.

Toyuk just nodded.

"Father—we love You. It's obvious You love this man; be with him as You send him to his home and to his next assignment. Help him see and hear what You want him to see and hear. Thank You Jesus, in Your Name we pray." Mark quickly grabbed Toyuk and hugged him. "In my dream I never learned your name. Would you allow me to know it so that I can pray for you as He directs and reminds me of you?"

"Toyuk," was all Toyuk could get out, as emotions were overwhelming him. "Thank you, sir," Toyuk said as Mark released him from the bear hug.

"I'm Mark. It's good to meet you, brother. Now I believe I'm supposed to give you a ride back to your home?"

"That would be helpful, thank you, Mark." Toyuk had never met anyone like Mark before, although there was something about Mark that made him feel comfortable with him like he felt with Ona and Miccoon..

"My truck is just down the street in the parking lot. Walk with me?" As they walked down the street Mark slipped into a coffee shop, Toyuk followed him inside. "What kind of coffee do you like?" Mark smiled at Toyuk. "I'm paying."

"Can I get a tea instead? Thank you so much." Toyuk was surprised at how he was feeling about Mark; he seemed like he was already family to him.

"You just step up to the counter and tell them what you want." Mark put his hand on Toyuk's shoulder and guided him in front of him.

On the ride back to the Peterson's home, Toyuk asked Mark all sorts of questions about spiritual things. Their conversation was easy and flowed as Mark explained his own personal walk and life with Jesus.

"I was chosen to do His work as a teenager, much like you, Toyuk. At 14 Jesus healed me of a terminal illness. The doctors told me and my parents that I could die soon—in days or as long as maybe 6 months." Mark paused and had a frown on his face. "The doctors wanted to get me on an experimental trial and procedure, but 50% of the people who try it die in the operation, and then they usually only live for another 2 years. I told my parents to take me home. I was tired of being the doctors' pincushion. My parents really wanted me to start the process of the trial, but still honored my wishes. So, I thought I'd just go home to die. I already knew Jesus, so I figured He'd just take me home." Mark smiled at Toyuk and nodded. "But to make this long story short, Jesus healed me, filled me with the Holy Spirit, and the doctors tried to figure out where my leukemia went for 3 years, but I just kept telling them that Jesus healed me. So, I've been on this roller coaster ride with Jesus and the Holy Spirit now for almost 48 years now. And I've lived longer than I expected. But every day is now His day, and not mine, as my life ended at 14 and His life and days began then … in me. Life with Jesus sure is an adventure." Mark chuckled.

Toyuk listened intently to Mark's story. And he knew Mark was telling him the truth. Toyuk pondered much of what Mark told him.

As Toyuk told Mark where to turn, they ended up in the Petersons' driveway. Just then the garage door opened. Stephanie was walking into the garage and saw the truck and Toyuk getting out of it. Mark also got out, seeing Stephanie in the garage. Mark waited by the side of his truck.

"Toyuk, who is this man?" Stephanie was sternly talking and looking at Toyuk and walking towards the truck.

"His name is Mark, he's my friend. The Great Spirit set up our meeting for this morning."

"Wait … what?" Stephanie looked at Toyuk, who was smiling and then to the older gentleman who was also smiling, and then she recognized him from the grocery store. "You!! You're the ... the... man who gave me the...message from God." Stephanie was still somewhat hesitant of Mark but wondering and also curious all at the same time.

"Yes, ma'am, I remember. Is this the boy? So God was referring to Toyuk then in the Word He wanted me to give you? Why, he's become a man now."

Toyuk smiled inside, here was a man, an elder, calling him a "man". It brought back a flood of memories of his manhood initiation. He wondered, pondered, and inwardly prayed, *"Great Spirit—did I really pass my initiation?"*

"Mark, I'm Stephanie. Can I get your contact information? I'm sure my husband Erik and I would like to talk with you further."

"That would be wonderful. My wife and I are new to town and would love to fellowship with those who love Jesus." Mark stepped forward, handing Stephanie a card and one to Toyuk. "I don't know how long you're still going to be around Toyuk, but you're welcome to call me anytime."

Stephanie glanced at Toyuk wondering what Mark meant by that.

"Goodbye, Toyuk, see you later! I would love to hear from you and your husband, but I've got another appointment to get to, so I'm off." Mark climbed back into the cab, as Stephanie and Toyuk walked into the garage.

"So, are you going to tell me what that was all about?" Stephanie was using her "mom" voice.

"The Great Spirit, or the Holy Spirit as Mark calls Him, woke me up early this morning and told me to meet a man. That man turned out to be Mark. I got a ride from Michael."

"And he didn't stay with you to meet this guy Mark?"

"I didn't tell Michael who the meeting was with, just that I had a meeting and needed a ride to the Tower District. I didn't know it was with Mark. The Great Spirit just told me what he looked like."

"This is all very strange." Stephanie stared at Toyuk. Toyuk just sat at the kitchen table quietly. "Soooo.... What was the message Mark was to give to you?"

"Did Mark already give you uh..., what was it he called it? A 'Word'? Before today? You've met him before? You never shared that with me." Toyuk was just calmly smiling at Stephanie as she peppered him with questions

"Don't change the subject, young man. What was the message?"

Toyuk paused. Sitting and listening and waiting for instructions from the Great Spirit. *"You can tell her, but you'll have to say it again for Erik, just so you know."*

"God gave a dream to Mark. In the dream there were instructions for Mark and a message for me. Mark didn't know my name, but he saw my face in the dream. So, he recognized me right away and gave me the message."

"And?" Stephanie said with a slight annoyed anticipation.

"The message basically was that I would be returning to my people," Toyuk said very plainly.

"Is that it? When? How? What are you supposed to do? What do you need to do to be ready? What do we need to do? What are you supposed to wear? Are you supposed to tell someone? How are you going to get there? Have you told anyone else? Do you trust this Mark guy?" Stephanie was talking fast and not letting Toyuk get a word in. But then she remembered the Word that Mark gave her in the supermarket about Toyuk. She paused, putting 2 + 2 together.

"I'm sure the Great Spirit will guide me as He sees my needs," Toyuk said quickly and calmly as Stephanie paused.

Just at that moment the Holy Spirit spoke to Toyuk in his mind, *"I've been giving dreams to Stephanie too."*

"Yes ... well... ah...." Stephanie was grasping on how to deal with this new information and entire situation.

"The Great Spirit just told me He's been giving you dreams too. Have you asked Him what they mean, what you're to do with them?" Toyuk said with curiosity in his voice.

"Um... well..." Stephanie didn't know how to respond as she hadn't even thought of the idea to ask the Holy Spirit about the strange dreams she had been having.

"Well, I prayed to God about the dreams ..." Stephanie was struggling. "The Great Spirit wants to guide us. He wants to help us. He will explain certain things to us if we are willing to listen, at least that's what I'm learning. I suggest you ask Him to help you understand."

Toyuk was very calm and spoke somewhat quietly. "The Great Spirit often sends me to the book you gave me to read on how He spoke to others through His Son, Jesus, and also to the letters in the book from the man called Paul for better understanding on how Jesus works and how the Holy Spirit works in us and through us. I'm still learning so much from that book. The Great Spirit is a good teacher. He helps me understand. But the book also gives me so many more questions to ask Him. The Great Spirit which I'm learning is a great mystery as He is more than one but three and still one." Toyuk paused to give Stephanie time to respond.

"Well ... Toyuk, I've been listening to sermons in Church all my life, but I've not learned anything that deals with... personal dreams like this. This... this... is all kinda new to me." Stephanie was slowing down in her talking and pondering what just came out of this strange boy/man who had entered so strangely into their lives. How was it that this person could know so much about God yet be such a "new" Christian? Yet—he knew and understood things that continually surprised her.

"I'm learning that the Great Spirit has been talking to me much longer than I understand, through dreams, through other people who love me, in the forest and lands, through situations I couldn't understand at the time. I still have so much to learn." Toyuk smiled at her.

Just then the door from the garage opened and Erik walked in.

"Um... someone left the garage door open." Erik looked at Stephanie and Toyuk, then began to realize that there was a pretty serious conversation going on.

"Toyuk has been meeting with strangers," Stephanie announced to Erik.

"Mark is no longer a stranger, plus you said he had already given you a message before." Toyuk looked back and forth at Erik and Stephanie."

"Who is Mark?" Erik was standing there looking confused.

"Mark is the stranger whom Toyuk met with this morning, and it seems he is the same guy that spoke to me at the supermarket."

"You mean the same guy who came to the hospital to deliver a message to me? That Mark? He seems to be getting around." Erik said slowly. "Soooo.... why did you meet with this Mark guy?" Erik was looking at Toyuk.

"The Great Spirit woke me up this morning to tell me where to go and that I would be meeting with someone who He gave a message to for me."

"And how did you get there?" Erik waiting.

"Michael." Toyuk was answering with less and less words.

"What did Michael think of Mark?"

"He didn't meet him. At least I don't think he has met Mark before, like you two have."

"Okay—I'll ask him later, so what was the message Mark gave you?"

"That I'd be returning to my people soon, and that I could only bring the book back with me."

"Wait, what?" Stephanie obviously heard the new information about the book.

"Why don't you give me a play by play from the beginning, Toyuk." Erik was slipping into his chaplain voice.

So Toyuk gave Erik and Stephanie a point-by-point description of his morning with Mark.

"I think we need to call this guy, Steph."

"And say what, Erik? Ask him what? Just unload our entire lives onto him? Ask this stranger how to deal with dreams? How do we know he isn't a Jim Jones kind of guy?"

"Who is Jim Jones?" Toyuk asked as he watched himself being edged out of the conversation.

"Never mind," both Stephanie and Erik said sharply at the same time at Toyuk.

"Can I go now?" Toyuk politely asked.

"Yeah, yeah, I gotta grab some food for lunch and get to the hospital. Steph, we'll talk about this when I get home."

Toyuk quietly got up and left while Steph followed Erik further into the kitchen. "This is all freaking me out a bit, Erik. I don't know how to make sense of much of this."

"Well, I definitely have to ponder this some." Erik was gathering food out of the fridge.

"Maybe we should pray about it? Maybe together?" Stephanie was thinking about her conversation with Toyuk.

Toyuk decided to get out of the house and head out to the barn. He wanted to spend some time with the Great Spirit and ask Him more questions, but he also just wanted to be in the quiet for a while. *Things are about to change again and soon*, I think. Toyuk needed time to ponder and think.

An unusual breeze was picking up and blowing through the barn. Toyuk was becoming aware of the Great Spirit's Presence more and more in His slight moving ways within him, and he began to feel more at peace.

What would you have me do, Great Spirit?

"Follow Me."

"Lead on," Toyuk actually said out loud.

Toyuk closed his eyes and stood still. He could feel the slight breeze across his face. Then he began to feel the wind shift, and new smells filled his nostrils.

He slowly opened his eyes.

He was no longer in the barn. He was standing next to an oak tree; the barn was gone, the house was gone. There was no sign of the world and time he was just in. There were no people in sight. Only an occasional bird call broke the silence. Toyuk looked around, there on a stone about 5 feet from him sat the book.

Toyuk walked over, picked up his Bible, and began walking towards the mountains. He wondered which time he was in now. He wondered if he was back in his time. But everything in him told him to walk to his old village spot in the mountains. It would take a few days to get there. He wished he had his old bow and water pouch with him. But all he had was the clothes on his back and his book.

"But now you have ME to guide you." The Holy Spirit whispered in Toyuk's mind. *"I'll show you where to go, and what to do. Don't worry, I've got you. Turn left at the three oaks and head for the river."*

As Toyuk approached what looked like three oak trees close together, he could see smoke from cooking fires in the distance off to his right on the valley floor several miles away.

Toyuk approached the river scanning for anyone who might be around; he seemed to be alone. As he looked at the river there on a rock near the water lay a water pouch, he quickly looked around again trying to see its owner. He waited for a good amount of time and no one came. He then remembered Miccoon's fishing lessons. *I wonder if I've still got the skills?* Toyuk decided he had nothing to lose and took off his shoes, socks, pants, shirt, and ventured into the river. He looked for any type of fish. As he was up to his waist in the river, he walked slowly up stream, with his hands submerged, ready to go. Several times he felt a fish go past but he was unable to catch them. *I must really relax and try to remember what Miccoon taught me.* Toyuk took a deep breath and stood still. He closed his eyes and waited, and it wasn't long and Toyuk had two trout.

It took a while since Toyuk hadn't made a fire in over 3 years in the native way, but by the evening he had a cooking fire and fish to eat, and water to drink.

Thank you Great Spirit! Toyuk was now firmly aware he was no longer alone; he had the One residing inside guiding him.

That night after finding a safe place to sleep, he slept with dreams of his past, nervous dreams, confrontative situations, and wrestling with his own doubts and fears.

12

REENTRY

The hike back towards the village was slow and difficult. Toyuk knew if he followed the river east into the mountains he would then come to familiar territory, but that also meant trying to stay out of sight of anyone else who might be at the river. He was having to make some pretty big detours to avoid individuals he saw in the distance.

By the third day after arriving back, Toyuk was pretty sure he was in his old timeline. The people's deerskin clothes he saw at a distance, the river, and mountains were looking very familiar. But he was still wearing 21st century clothing. Everything about him screamed "different" now. His haircut, his shoes, nothing about his appearance fit into this place and time.

Toyuk was asking the Great Spirit for advice on how to re-enter his village. What was he supposed to say? How was he supposed to explain his disappearance and his reappearance after these years? He was imagining all sorts of reactions. He wondered what everyone was doing now. *Did Nea already have a child already with Kinar?* He wondered how his mom was doing. He knew his disappearance must have been really hard on her. So many things, situations, and people Toyuk pondered about as he hiked into the mountains.

Toyuk had changed greatly while living 3 years millennia in the future. He had grown tremendously physically. He was much bigger and stronger than he was just 3 years ago. The vast quantities of food he had had available and gotten used to eating, and daily workouts and protein supplements with Michael had put significant muscles on his body. He also had grown over ten inches in the last three years, and he didn't realize now that he was taller than the average man at this time. Between his height and changes in his body, as well as his haircut and clothing, he figured no one would recognize him ... at first.

The sun had gone down but Toyuk was now in familiar territory. It was all coming back to him now. He had been walking in the dark for some time, but his eyes had adjusted, and he was recognizing more and more as he hiked towards his village.

All of a sudden Toyuk was hit in the head from behind by a rock, and the world faded away. When he awoke, he was being dragged. His hands and feet were bound while he was trying to make out the man who was dragging him, but he couldn't tell much as his captor was pulling Toyuk by his feet with his back to him. Soon Toyuk could see others coming. With a couple of war cries, soon the whole village was awake and coming out of their dwellings.

"Leto?" Toyuk was catching the face of his captor.

Leto stopped and drew closer to Toyuk's face. "How do you know my name, outsider?" Leto was menacing in his question.

"Leto, I'm Toyuk."

"Toyuk is dead."

"Obviously not. I'm back."

By then most of the village was gathered around looking at this very strangely dressed captive. They were surprised he spoke their language and were whispering among each other.

"Who are you, and what do you want? Don't you know it's very dangerous to approach us after the sun has set?" Kinar had stepped forward and was directly pointing at Toyuk with his questions.

"Where is Tregor? I'd like to speak to Tregor." Toyuk wanted to speak to the entire village at once, trying to avoid countless interrogations by each native warrior before finally getting to speak to the leader of the tribe.

"I am chief now. Answer my questions," Kinar said with sternness.

"Kinar..."

Kinar was surprised that this stranger knew his name and became even more wary.

"... I'm Toyuk. I know from Leto that everyone thought I was dead when I didn't come back from the initiation hunt. But my story is long and difficult to explain."

"You have entered our territory unannounced and you will tell me in the morning why you have invaded our village." Kinar made the pronouncement. "Leto, take this man to the boundary tree. Buldar, you will stand guard to make sure he doesn't escape."

Toyuk quickly tried to find the face of his best friend. Then a shorter stocky man came forward and began helping Leto pull Toyuk to the tree.

"Buldar, is that you?" Toyuk was soft in his question to his friend.

"I don't know you," Buldar replied curtly.

"Yes, you do, my friend. I know it's been a long time..." Toyuk was warm in his voice.

"You will be quiet and not speak! You will not move if you want to live!"

Toyuk was trying to get through to his friend but was being ignored. Buldar was busy tying him to the tree, and after he finished, he moved out of voice range and sat down and stared at him. Leto just walked away.

It was a long night for Toyuk. Being tied to the boundary tree didn't make sleep easy. In the morning dawn Toyuk could see the village coming to life. So many memories flooded his mind.

He looked hard for his mom's dwelling, but some of the dwellings had moved and some were just gone. A few new dwellings also had been put up. Still, he couldn't see his mom anywhere. He also was hoping to see Miccoon and Ona. He thought he caught a glimpse of them on the very far side of the village, but he wasn't sure.

Then he saw Tregor. Toyuk was confused as the man was a shell of the strong leader Toyuk remembered. Tregor moved slowly and looked like he had lost weight. Toyuk then saw Nayee as she busied herself with getting the morning cooking fire going.

The village was busy with their morning chores. They all seemed to ignore the man tied to the boundary tree. Leto then approached Buldar, and Buldar got up and left with Leto taking his place.

⤞———————⤞

It was about midday, when Kinar approached Toyuk. Kinar ordered Leto to drag the prisoner to the center of the village. By the time Leto had gotten Toyuk to the village center, the entire tribe had gathered. All eyes were now on Toyuk.

"You will now speak," Kinar said with authority as he cut the rope from Toyuk's hands. Kinar then went and sat down in the chief's spot.

Toyuk could see Rohue sitting next to Kinar. Toyuk prayed in his mind to the Holy Spirit. *Please give me the right words to say. Help me to know what to say and what not to say.*

"Just begin at the beginning, I'll let you know when to stop or not say something. Trust Me," the Holy Spirit spoke gently in Toyuk's mind.

Thank you for being with me, Toyuk responded in his mind.

"I'm Toyuk. I know almost all of you, and you know me. I would like to see my mother Shushe. Is she here?"

Just then he saw Ona gasp, and cover her mouth, Miccoon cocked his head.

"You will speak and tell us why we should not kill you, outsider. We will not answer any of your questions till you have explained yourself," Kinar spoke firmly, but he was noticing others in the village whispering more and more to one another.

"I will tell all of you my story. Obviously, it begins with my initiation with my friends Buldar, Leto, Yellot, and the others. I was blessed to catch some fish on my first day of the final trial, and roast a rabbit on my second day, but as everyone knows a buck is the prize we all wanted, so I went to the little lakes to see if the herd would be there. I saw three does at the small lake and decided to wait for the morning to see if a buck would also show up. While I was thinking about the best place to wait for the best shot, I began to maneuver towards the large rocks to find a good vantage point. As I came towards the rocks, I noticed there was a light coming from around the largest rock. The sun had just set so the light was strange to me. As I went to find what was making this light, when I came around the rock, the light blinded me, it was so bright. The light dimmed somewhat, and I was able to see what it was." Toyuk paused. He knew good storytelling techniques. He waited till everyone was looking at him and listening intently, waiting for him to continue.

"I think this really is Toyuk," Ona whispered to Miccoon, while Toyuk was telling the first part of his story.

Toyuk continued. "The light was coming from.... a great white buck." Toyuk could see Rohue's reaction. Rohue had leaned in. "I stood still. I must admit I was afraid, and I didn't know what to do..." Toyuk knew admitting his fear is something a warrior is his tribe did not do. "But then a Voice spoke to me, and said, 'Rise and kill!' So... I raised my bow to shoot when my foot slipped and I fell. When I fell, I must have hit my head because I awoke in another...time."

The tribe began to whisper rapidly with one another. Toyuk watched Rohue lean in and say something to Kinar.

"Where is your bow now? Where is Tonuw's knife?" Kinar asked Toyuk, and the other tribe members quieted themselves in order to hear Toyuk's response.

"I don't have them. I don't know if they are still there." Toyuk had not considered that his bow and father's knife could still be at the rock outcropping at the small lake of the little lakes. This question made him want to go back to try and find them. *Would they still be there after three years?* Toyuk wondered.

"I found Toyuk's bow Kinar .. remember?" Leto spoke up.

"It was after we went looking for Shushe. But no one found Tonuw's knife," Buldar said.

Buldar had been listening to Toyuk intently looking to see if he could see anything of his friend Toyuk in this stranger. Toyuk's voice and mannerisms were more and more reminding him of his boyhood best friend. But this man was so much bigger than Toyuk; he was even bigger than Tonuw used to be and even taller now than Buldar. And this man looked strong, but his skin coverings were so strange. His sandals were the strangest foot coverings Buldar had ever seen.

"No one found Shushe." Buldar looked straight at Toyuk with a stern face when he said this.

"Where did the 'great white buck' take you?" Kinar cut in before Toyuk could respond.

"*I am with you*," The Holy Spirit said gently and lovingly in Toyuk's mind.

Toyuk began speaking, but tears were forming in his eyes. "Actually I don't know. I think it wasn't a 'where' but a 'when'. I think the Great Spirit took me to another... time. To the place where I had seen in my dreams." Toyuk saw Ona nod her head. "When I returned to this village—it wasn't here. There were more trees and fallen logs all through this area. I found the grinding holes near the river, but the river had changed too ... in many ways. I remembered the discussion about maybe moving to the foothills to begin planting, so I began walking down the mountain to find you." Toyuk moved his hands, motioning them to the entire tribe. "On my walk down the mountain I encountered a tall stiff net which I climbed to get over, but at the top I touched something that put me to sleep. When I awoke this time, I was exactly where my dreams had me many times. On a flat surface with wide ropes, being held down by them and surrounded by people who were very pale, and wearing skins I only had seen in my dreams and speaking a language I didn't know. They would stick me, and I would sleep more."

"*Tell them of Erik and Stephanie and living with them, but that I then brought you back. Don't say anything more at this time.*" The Holy Spirit had spoken very clearly in Toyuk's mind.

While listening to the Holy Spirit, Toyuk had closed his eyes and took a deep breath.

"I was taken to live with a new tribe in that time. The warrior's name is 'Erik' and his wife's name is 'Stephanie'."

The weird sounding names brought again the whispers among the tribe members.

"The Great Spirit taught me many things while I was there, but then He said He was going to bring me back. So here I am. Will you allow me to search for my father's knife? Buldar and Leto can go with me so you know I won't betray you."

Just then Rohue spoke up. "I'm very intrigued by your story. The great White Buck is nothing to be played with. The great White Buck is a sacred spirit. This encounter needs to be verified."

Kinar then gave his orders. "Buldar and Leto... you will take this man to look for Tonuw's knife. Do not let him escape or trick you."

The tribe members began to rise, as Buldar and Leto went to get Toyuk to his feet which they untied, and then the tribe began to disperse and go about their day.

Ona and Miccoon stayed to watch this man. Ona began walking to the three. Toyuk saw Ona and stopped moving. Buldar and Leto then noticed Ona approaching them.

Ona came straight up to Toyuk and threw her arms around him and whispered in his ear. "Welcome home son. I believe you." Ona then let go of Toyuk and turned to Buldar. "Buldar, wait here while I get Toyuk some water. He'll need it for the hike."

Toyuk's mouth was already dry from not having any water the entire night and morning. Toyuk's eyes were now leaking tears as Ona's words were sinking into his heart. Ona returned with a water pouch and Toyuk took it with so much gratitude.

"Thank you, Ona." After almost emptying the entire pouch, Toyuk turned and said to Buldar and Leto, "Let's go find my father's knife."

Buldar and Leto looked at each other, both wondering more and more if this man was their old friend Toyuk.

The three men began the long hike to the little lakes. At the beginning they were all silent, with Buldar and Leto following Toyuk. Leto had tied a rope around Toyuk like a leash.

"What happened to Tregor?" Toyuk broke the silence.

"Tregor was never the same after Nea's accident," Buldar spoke plainly.

"What accident?" Toyuk was now finally getting some more information.

"During the initiation Nea broke her leg badly. It never set well. She now walks with a very bad limp. Kinar chose another. No other warrior wanted Nea. Tregor and Nayee gave almost everything they had to Rohue to help fix Nea. Tregor and

Rohue no longer talk to each other. Kinar is now our tribe leader." Buldar didn't expound on the story but just gave quick facts.

"You never were a good storyteller, Buldar," Toyuk said quietly.

Leto snickered.

"You walk," Buldar said gruffly. And then under his breath, "You are the one who left me. I didn't leave you or my mom."

Toyuk heard Buldar's quiet statement and then responded. "So you do believe I am who I say I am."

"My friend Toyuk left us long ago. If you are Toyuk, I don't know you now. You just walk."

The three walked in silence for the next miles to the little lakes area. Toyuk turned at the smaller lake and headed towards the rock outcropping. When they arrived Toyuk began to speak out loud about his movements from that initiation day. "I came around this rock when I saw the light. Then I walked to the crack and the opening."

The two followed Toyuk.

"When I tried to shoot, I was standing up there." Toyuk pointed to a rock. "I then fell... and landed somewhere near here." Toyuk was now on his hands and knees, looking and moving through the pine needles at the base of a huge ponderosa pine tree. Then there it was hidden under some pine needles. Toyuk lifted the knife to Buldar.

Thank you... Holy Spirit! Toyuk was praising the Great Spirit in his heart and mind.

Buldar took the knife from Toyuk and turned it over and over, remembering how Toyuk had lent the knife to him during the initiation trials for a brief time. He definitely recognized it.

"Alright. Let's go back." Buldar wasn't celebrating at all; in fact he seemed angry at Toyuk to Leto.

"I guess there actually is something to your story," Leto said to Toyuk. "I'm not sure what wasp got under your skins, Buldar," Leto said jokingly.

"Shut up, Leto. Keep a watch on him." Buldar was in a foul mood.

Toyuk began an internal conversation with the Holy Spirit as they walked back to the village.

What's wrong with Buldar?

"He's still hurt and wounded from when I took you long ago." The answer was gentle from the Holy Spirit. *"He has many wounds that are now twisted within him. You need to pray for him."*

Toyuk knew the Holy Spirit was giving him some insider information that only He knew.

I will pray for him, starting right now. "Great Spirit please reveal Yourself to my friend Buldar. Please work in his life. Great Spirit I want him to encounter Your Son Jesus like I did."

Toyuk could actually feel the Holy Spirit's emotions as he prayed for Buldar. He could tell that the Great Spirit loved Buldar very much.

Toyuk could also sense that his reentry to the tribe wasn't going to be an easy one. He hoped that finding his father's knife would help people to believe him. And he was also concerned about his friend Buldar, and if he would be able to reestablish a friendship with him. Toyuk continued to pray all the way back. He found that the Holy Spirit was giving him names of tribe members to pray for and exactly what to pray about for each member. It was a new experience for Toyuk as he pondered the secrets the Holy Spirit was revealing about so many in the tribe.

As they entered the village, Buldar went immediately to his dwelling, leaving Toyuk with Leto just holding the rope.

Kinar made his way to Toyuk and Leto. "Did you find the knife?"

"Toyuk found it. Buldar has it now." Leto was still standing and holding the rope.

"Where is Buldar?" Kinar was stern.

"I think he went to his dwelling," Leto replied.

Toyuk was quiet just watching and listening—listening to more than just the conversation in front of him.

"Leave this man here and go get Buldar," Kinar ordered.

Leto passed the rope to Kinar and then sprinted off in the direction of Buldar's dwelling. Kinar dropped the rope.

"Sit down. Don't move." Kinar was still not friendly in any way.

But at least I'm not tied to anyone right now, Toyuk thought. The Holy Spirit was telling Toyuk just to be patient and still.

What's next? inquired Toyuk in his mind.

"This is going to take a while. Be patient. Listen to Me. Don't do anything I haven't told you to do." The Holy Spirit was very clear in Toyuk's mind.

Toyuk just then remembered his Bible was still somewhere out there. But at least it was in this... time. He was determined to find it before someone else did.

13

TRIBAL DECISION

Nayee looked at Tregor and said in a hushed voice, "What do you think of the outsider's story? Do you think that man is actually Toyuk?"

Tregor responded quietly, "Everything I've been seeing, and hearing doesn't strike me as suspicious. The only thing that makes me wary are the weird skins he is wearing, and his hair is so short, which we all know is a form of punishment and shame."

"Nea has been listening and watching too, I think she wants to talk to the outsider." Nayee said. Tregor then said, "I'm leaning in believing his story, just because it is so different, as is his skins. But I want to wait before allowing Nea any time with him. We aren't in a good position already, and we have to be careful."

Tregor and Nayee made sure their voices were at almost a whisper for the conversation. They had become so weary and wary of anything they said or did in the tribe now. Rohue and Kinar had taken over, and their position in the tribe was very precarious currently.

⇒——————⇒

"Do you have the knife?" Kinar was confronting Buldar as he and Leto were walking towards him.

Toyuk sat silently watching the exchange. He had also been watching all of the other tribe members and been taking mental notes.

"Yes I have *a* knife," Buldar replied.

"Is it Tonuw's knife?" Kinar looked at him with narrowed eyes.

"It might be." Buldar knew fully well it was Tonuw's old knife.

"Leto... you saw it, yes? What say you?" Kinar was not liking Buldar's reaction and answers.

"I never got to see the knife before, so I can't say, but by the reaction of the outsider, or Toyuk if he is who he says he is, I think the knife is Tonuw's." Leto glanced at Buldar. Buldar had more of his scowl on his face than normal. His usual face always carried a scowl and people tended to not engage with Buldar in polite talk.

"Go and bring it here. NOW!" Kinar almost shouted. He was loud enough to turn people's heads to see what the commotion was.

Buldar gruffly turned and walked and Leto ran in the direction of Buldar's dwelling.

"Why are you holding back, Buldar? I saw your face when you held the knife; you recognized it." Leto was trying to get Buldar to explain as he waited by Buldar's dwelling.

"I have my reasons," Buldar snapped back and went into his dwelling.

Buldar emerged from the dwelling and began walking back to Kinar, Leto following behind. "Here." Buldar stuck out the knife.

Just then Miccoon began to walk to the group. His pace was slower than Toyuk remembered and he looked older than he had ever seen him. But he held his head high and walked with dignity. Kinar and the group stopped and waited for Miccoon to greet them.

"Chief." Miccoon stopped in front of Kinar just past where Toyuk was sitting on the ground. "I believe there is some evidence now to this man's story. May I see it?"

Kinar handed the knife to Miccoon. Miccoon turned it over and over in his hands, looking at the handle, blade, carving, and binding.

"Yes, this was Tonuw's knife. I can confirm it," Miccoon said with certainty.

Toyuk actually felt some brief relief. But he was surprised when Miccoon directly turned around and walked back to his dwelling without even acknowledging Toyuk. He wondered what Miccoon thought of him; he so wanted to just talk with Miccoon. He missed him greatly, and now being back he just wanted to get back to life and reestablish the relationships with those he loved.

"*Patience, Toyuk.*" The Holy Spirit was gentle in His tone in Toyuk's mind.

Toyuk began to take deep breaths and slowly let them out. It was his way of centering himself, focusing, and relaxing.

"You may go." Kinar waved his hand at Buldar and Leto, and they turned and walked away. "So, Toyuk, what do I do with you now? I was barely aware of you before, and you were a nothing kid. You definitely are an outsider now." Kinar was talking more to himself than to Toyuk, although he wanted Toyuk to know what he thought of him. Kinar thought he needed to talk to Rohue about strategy and what to do with the problem of this ... outsider... Toyuk. "Stay here. Don't move," Kinar ordered Toyuk. He walked off to find Rohue.

As she watched Kinar walk off, Nayee walked by Toyuk and slipped him a water pouch. As she stood with her back to Toyuk she whispered, "Tregor and I believe that you are Toyuk."

Toyuk made a hand sign that meant "thank you." He knew that he couldn't engage in a conversation with her out in the open.

Nayee turned and walked back to her dwelling.

"What are you doing?!" Tregor asked her quietly and sternly as she entered their dwelling.

"By now he must be thirsty. This tribe is not very welcoming anymore."

Kinar found Rohue and motioned him to his dwelling. As they got inside, he began the questioning.

"Rohue, how do we deal with this problem outsider who calls himself Toyuk?"

"We have to be careful with this situation. It's going to take some wise strategy on your part." Rohue was speaking submissively and overly sweet to Kinar.

"What do you suggest, Rohue?"

"I think we need to have the elders make the decision we want and will give you the best position on the matter."

"And how do we do that exactly?"

Rohue was silent as his mind was spinning with strategies. Then he began to smile ever so slightly. "Call an elders' council. Since Shushe is no longer with us, Toyuk must be placed with another warrior, as Toyuk officially never completed the initiation ritual. I think that Toyuk should be placed with Tregor and Nayee. Let's keep the problems in one area." Rohue made these statements slow and methodical.

"I like the way you think, Rohue. I will call for a council tonight."

The afternoon wore on, and the sun was warm. Toyuk sat in the middle of the village, working on his... patience. Ona walked by and Toyuk suddenly found a corn cake dropped in his lap. He made no move or sound to alert anyone of what just happened. He turned slightly to look in the direction of her dwelling and saw Miccoon just inside the flap giving him the "calm" hand sign.

That night the elders had gathered for the council meeting. They sat just outside of Kinar's dwelling around a fire. Rohue began the meeting.

"We have a problem all of you know about. It is this outsider who calls himself Toyuk. His story is intriguing, and there may be some evidence that supports his story, but as to his identity ... well, that hasn't been fully established yet."

"Shaman," Miccoon spoke as Rohue paused after his opening statement. "I can confirm that the knife I inspected was Tonuw's knife."

"Yes, Miccoon, Kinar told me this, thank you for your wisdom and memory." Rohue was ever so ingratiating in his tone. Rohue continued, "As a matter of tribal tradition and protocol we must remember if this really is Toyuk, he did not actually complete his manhood initiation ritual to be part of the men of this tribe. The tradition would indicate that he still must be under another warrior until such time he can pass the trials again. Do we have anyone who will take this Toyuk into their dwelling?"

"I will." Miccoon spoke clearly.

"Thank you, Miccoon. Your wisdom and loyalty to this tribe is marked again this night." Kinar was speaking with authority. "But it is also my task to see to the health, welfare, and security of this entire tribe. You and Ona are extremely valuable members and your wisdom and experience is sorely needed. I will not place any more burden on either of you at this time. I think Toyuk needs a seasoned warrior with family and leadership experience to watch over him and guide him in the ways of our traditions. This is why I am choosing Tregor for this honor." Kinar was speaking with clarity and seemingly humility.

Tregor immediately knew this was a scheme of Rohue's. But he also knew he couldn't refuse. So Tregor resolved to go with it. "If it is your wisdom for Toyuk to stay with myself and Nayee, we will do it with honor for our tribe."

"Thank you, Tregor. Do all of you agree?"

The elders all motioned acceptance except Miccoon.

"Then it is settled, you will take Toyuk tonight." Kinar waved his hand and the council meeting was over.

On the way back to his dwelling, Tregor walked past Toyuk and said, "Come with me."

Toyuk got up and followed Tregor. He was surprised when Tregor went straight to his dwelling and pushed back the flap and walked in. Toyuk followed and stood just inside.

"Our honor is to take Toyuk into our dwelling and family for the tribe," Tregor announced to everyone who was now staring at Toyuk.

Nayee pulled Tregor aside. "What's this all about? Another large mouth to feed? I do believe this is Toyuk, but...."

"Nayee—I will do my best to supply this family with all of my skills and talents so that this family will prosper," Toyuk spoke quietly and clearly. Toyuk's eyes were adjusting as he looked around the dwelling. The younger kids were there watching Toyuk intently, and then he saw her. She was sitting in the corner. She looked so different. Her hair was very short. Her face looked skinny. Her skins looked loose on her. "Hello, Nea."

"Is that really you?" Nea asked from the dark corner.

"Yes. I've wondered about you over the past years, Nea."

"As you can see, much has changed," Nea said quietly with a hint of bitterness.

"Toyuk, until we can make an addition to this shelter, you will sleep in this corner." Tregor motioned to a far corner opposite of where Nea was.

"I will get started on the addition tomorrow, as well as get some fresh fish for Nayee. Don't worry, Tregor, I will help you provide for this family." Toyuk was speaking as sincerely with honor as he could. "Perhaps you could show me where the best trees are for making a new bow and arrows? You were my teacher and have great wisdom with a bow. I look forward to learning from you again."

Tregor nodded, thinking maybe this situation won't be as bad as Rohue wanted it to be. *Toyuk looks strong and willing, maybe my family will prosper again.*

"Tregor, may I go sit outside? I want to think." Toyuk acknowledged Tregor's hand motion and slipped outside.

Toyuk sat outside and prayed.

Jesus, help me to know what You want me to do. Thank You for all of the Holy Spirit's advice. Wait, do I thank You or the Holy Spirit? But you are One. The Great Spirit is still so much a mystery to me, but I want to understand You more. Help me now to tell Your story to this family, this tribe. Protect the Bible that came with me; please help me find it again. What do You want me to do now?

"*Just keep praying. I love you, Toyuk.*" Toyuk's eyes filled with tears. He could feel the love of the Great Spirit, Jesus, and the Creator. It felt like waves washing over his body. Waves of love, joy, and peace.

Just then Nea sat down next to him. It startled Toyuk. Nea could see the tears on Toyuk's face. "Are you okay?"

"Just having a chat with the Great Spirit," Toyuk said quietly.

"You speak with the Great Spirit?!" Nea said quietly and had a shocked look on her face.

"As you can see, much has changed," Toyuk playfully replied.

"Are you a Shaman now?" Nea was still trying to understand who Toyuk was now.

"I don't know, Nea. I'm certainly not a Shaman the way our tradition thinks of a Shaman. I'm just someone who is still trying to find his way in this world. I'm learning that the Great Spirit has a purpose for me, and has been preparing me for what... I don't know."

"Where were you, where did you go?"

Toyuk couldn't help noticing Nea's leg and that it was still needing help from some kind of accident. Toyuk sighed. "Nea… I don't know exactly where I went since I think it was more of *when* I went. This spot where this village is now—was still here, just different. No one was here. Our tribe was gone."

"You tried to find us?"

"Right away. I didn't care about the trials at that time, just that I wanted to be… home. I don't remember if I told you that I was having dreams when I was young and here before."

"I heard your mom and Ona talking about them." Nea was quiet in her voice.

"Well, in that place that I just came from—it was the place in my dreams. Many things in my dreams I didn't understand at all, but now I do. I learned a new place, family, tribe, language, and things I can't really describe to you now. It is a much more different place than here. I was an outsider there too."

"Sounds scary."

"It was. So many times, I was scared beyond what I thought possible."

"How did you survive?"

"Survive? Interesting—I see now how far these places are apart. There in that place there is always more food than one can eat. Surviving is different there, not like here. There I learned to listen to the Great Spirit. He began to speak to me more clearly at that place."

"Speak to you? The Great Spirit speaks to you?"

"And the Great Spirit wants to talk to you too, Nea."

Nea got very quiet. She turned her head away from Toyuk. "The Great Spirit hates me. That's why my father is no longer Chief. That's why I have a leg that doesn't work and causes every man to flee from me."

"I'm not fleeing from you, Nea. I want to know you better," Toyuk spoke gently.

"I'm ugly now." Nea kept her head down and looked away from Toyuk.

"I want always to be honest with you, Nea, as much as I can, but I also want to be direct with you and not hold any thoughts back. It's something I was learning in the other place. The wife of the warrior I was staying with was teaching me those ways. So, I just want to ask you this question—why is your hair so short now?"

"My father said that cutting it off was an offering Rohue needed to make to the spirits so that they would fix my leg. At least it's grown back some now," Nea said very quietly. "The spirits hate me. My leg hasn't changed."

Toyuk could hear the hurt. "I don't know about the other spirits, but I do know the Great Spirit loves you. I'm still learning, and have even more to learn than I know, but the Great Spirit is guiding me. When I can... I want to tell you everything I am learning and have learned."

Nea slowly turned to face Toyuk. "You would teach me?"

"Yes, I do want to teach you if you would like me to. And sometime when you are ready, I would like to hear from you the story of how your leg was injured. I will share with you my stories of the other place, and I can listen to your stories of this place and what I missed."

"I would like that." Nea slowly got up and went back into the dwelling. There was the smallest bit of hope that had been planted into Nea. She could feel something inside of her heart and it was... changing her.

Just then Toyuk heard a sound to the left of him. He looked and behind a tree just beyond the dwellings he could see just a bit of a woman. From her skins he could tell it was Ona. Toyuk got up and slowly began to walk towards the tree. He remembered the log where he and Ona had discussed his dreams years ago. When he got to the log, which Toyuk wondered if it would still be there, there sat Ona.

"My, how you have grown, Toyuk." There was a twinkle in the eyes of Ona.

Oh, how Toyuk loved this woman. Toyuk grabbed Ona and hugged her.

"Now that was a surprise. Very un-warrior like Toyuk." Ona winked at him. "I have something for you." Ona reached behind her and brought out a pair of skins. "They were an old pair of Miccoon's but they are a little big on him now, and I thought these might help you feel like your home, at least a little bit."

"I'm glad it's getting dark. My eyes are watering too much." Toyuk choked back the tears.

"You know I want to hear all about the adventures the Great Spirit took you on, but for now... just know that Miccoon and I will support you as we can. The Great Spirit will find a place and time for us to talk, of that I am certain." Ona got up and walked back towards the village and her dwelling.

Great Spirit, thank You for Ona! Toyuk was beginning to feel that he wasn't as alone as it seemed at first. Tregor, Nayee, Nea, and now Ona and Miccoon? *Thank You, Jesus.*

Toyuk walked back to Tregor and Nayee's dwelling with the bundle Ona had given him under his arm. Toyuk didn't want to wake anyone in the dwelling so he lay down next to the flap and put the skins under his head. He was tired, and sleep came quickly.

14

—— ◆ ——

HEALING

Toyuk was awakened and tripped over by running children out of Tregor's dwelling. *Should have remembered to sleep away from the flap. I did the same thing as a kid almost every morning.*

Toyuk got up and waved to the kids who were quickly picking themselves up and heading to the river. He went around the back of the dwelling, found some tall bushes, and quickly changed into Miccoon's old skins. He wrapped up his modern clothes and shoes in a bundle and dropped them off inside the dwelling. He nodded to Nayee and Nea before going out to find Tregor. He found Tregor coming back with a rabbit and a squirrel that he had just killed with a bow.

Tregor stopped and looked at Toyuk wearing Miccoon's old skins and nodded in approval. "Your hair still betrays you."

"There's nothing I can do about that now, Tregor. It will just take time. I see your skills with the bow have not diminished, Tregor. I will listen to your wisdom and training in these skills. I hope to find good materials for the addition to the dwelling today. Your family needs privacy; I respect that."

"And I will show you where you can find a good source for a new bow and arrows."

"I am honored, Tregor. Having my father's old knife would help me."

"I will see about getting it returned to you. I will take Miccoon and we will visit Kinar."

Toyuk nodded, and hand-signed thank you. He then turned and walked to find limbs and bark for the addition to the dwelling.

Tregor and Miccoon sat at the fire just outside the Chief's dwelling. When Kinar emerged, he looked at the two elders and sat down across from them. He was quickly served warm tea from his first wife, who came and went silently.

"We have come to ask for Tonuw's knife," Tregor stated plainly. Miccoon looked stoic at Kinar.

"It is safe," Kinar replied.

"It has been established the knife was Tonuw's. It has been accepted that the man is Toyuk, by you placing him with Tregor." Miccoon was very direct.

Kinar spoke firmly, "Wife!" Two women appeared at the flap. "Bring me Tonuw's knife." Kinar spoke dismissively and down at Tregor. "Tregor you are still responsible for anything the outsider causes. If he uses the knife unwisely, you will have to account."

Tregor nodded. The first woman reappeared holding the knife outstretched in her hand. Miccoon got up, signed thank you, and took the knife from her. Tregor and Miccoon walked away from the fire not saying another word.

While they walked back, Miccoon handed Tregor the knife. "Toyuk will need this. He has much work to do."

"Miccoon, I respect your wisdom. You are welcome to help guide Toyuk as you see fit."

Miccoon nodded. He had never had a close relationship with Tregor but was seeing him in a new light.

"Toyuk looks good in your skins."

"Ona is very generous. She loves Toyuk," Miccoon said quietly.

Miccoon and Tregor then walked in different directions.

Toyuk's feet were not used to being barefoot again. The old calluses on the souls of his feet were long gone. Three years of wearing shoes had made his feet soft.

He walked gingerly through the forest looking for limbs and bark suitable for the addition.

While looking for the materials for the addition, the Holy Spirit was gentle and soft in the mind of Toyuk.

Turn left. Toyuk was learning just to obey Him. He thought maybe the Holy Spirit would guide him to the materials.

After walking a distance, the Holy Spirit spoke again. *Now straight and walk thirty-two steps.* Toyuk began to count his steps. At the last step he stopped and looked around. There were no branches or bark anywhere near him. Toyuk was puzzled.

Look right. Go to the large sugar pine tree. Toyuk went to the pine tree.

Behind the stone. Toyuk looked for a stone. He saw a large rock behind the tree. There between the tree and the stone lay the Bible.

A flood of emotions came over Toyuk. Toyuk picking up the Bible brought feelings of home as he opened it and began to read. It fell open to Psalms 23. Toyuk loved the stories of David, the great warrior-king. He so looked forward to the many lessons the Holy Spirit would teach him from the Bible. He carefully tucked the Bible inside his skins, wondering where he should keep it when I got back to the dwelling. *Thank you, Holy Spirit!*

While Toyuk was walking back he saw a large downed tree with great branches that would be just right for the addition. Toyuk came dragging three large branches back with him. He then set about breaking them into the sizes he wanted. He had learned this by breaking them over a stone with just the right force. He was surprised how much easier it was now. His strength abilities were greatly enhanced by his physical growth over the last three years. He saw Tregor bringing large pieces of bark from another direction.

As Tregor met Toyuk, he held out the knife. "This should help."

Toyuk smiled and nodded. Then they both began to work on the new section of the addition.

Toyuk made the addition with an opening to the main dwelling as well as an opening to the outside. The corner where Tregor had chosen Toyuk to sleep was carefully taken apart to allow an opening to the new addition. By late afternoon the addition was almost complete.

At least I'll be able to sleep in it tonight, he thought to himself. He then thought that Nayee might want to have some fresh fish for dinner, and he ran down to the river.

He had caught and cleaned five trout and brought them to Nayee as she was at the family's cooking fire.

"Thank you, Toyuk, these will be nice alongside the rabbit stew."

"I always enjoyed my mom's way of seasoning the fish. I look forward to tasting yours."

"I know Gnut will appreciate the fresh fish. That boy has a bottomless stomach." Nayee was beginning to like having Toyuk around.

"Whenever you want fresh fish, you just let me know." Toyuk then signed thank you with his hands.

Toyuk is respectful, thoughtful, and handsome except for his hair, but then Nea's hair... I wonder if ... Nea... Nayee's thoughts were thinking of the future. *Best not go there just yet.* Nayee called out to Toyuk, "Be back soon, dinner is almost ready."

Toyuk turned and nodded in appreciation to Nayee.

Over the next few days, Toyuk worked and completed the addition, and Tregor had shown Toyuk the best trees for a new bow. He helped Toyuk fashion a bow of quality that was better than Toyuk had seen before, very much like the one Tregor himself used. Ona brought Toyuk some sandals after seeing Toyuk applying the skin healing juice from a plant to his feet. Miccoon had been showing Toyuk his new best fishing spots farther south on the river and reminding him of the best ways to make arrows and even provided him with some excellent arrow heads. Of course, Ona had been slipping her honey corn cakes to Miccoon to give to Toyuk every time he went out. Ona and Nayee had also been talking more and sharing recipes. Both seemed to be enjoying one another's company as the days went by.

Toyuk used the late afternoons to go off by himself to read and be taught by the Holy Spirit from his Bible. He could sense that the calm he was experiencing these days wouldn't last forever—that there would be a future confrontation and spiritual battle that would take place. Where, when, and with whom he wasn't quite sure about, but he had his suspicions.

Toyuk was becoming the evening's storyteller to Tregor's family. He used stories from the Bible as his source of his evening tales. The children sat enraptured by all of the new stories Toyuk was telling and were actually willing to get ready for sleep if Toyuk was going to tell a new story.

Of course, Tregor, Nayee, and Nea listened in, too. Tregor pondered the stories of the Great Spirit's creation of this world. And the snake's betrayal and deception. And then of the man named Noah and the Great Spirit's instructions of creating a large boat that took longer than a man's life in their time. So many stories, so much new information and concepts and lessons to think about and ponder. Nayee and Nea also were pondering Toyuk's evening stories.

But it was the stories about the Great Spirit's Son who had been sent into this world so that they all could know the Great Spirit for themselves, and that this Son named Jesus had actually spoken to Toyuk in the place where the Great Spirit had taken him during the three years, which had all of them feeling very different about the Great Spirit, especially learning of the great war in the heavens and how a third of the spirits went along with one like the snake who wanted to sit on the Great Spirit's place—that there were actually spirits that wanted to harm them, and that those spirits were actually against the Great Spirit and His faithful warriors. Nea actually cried when hearing Toyuk tell the story of Jesus and how He gave his life for them and died on that tree. The next night Toyuk told the story of Jesus coming out of His grave, everyone was wide-eyed.

Nea was especially interested in all of the stories about Jesus healing the sick, the lame, the blind, and even the spirit possessed. She pondered if Jesus wanted her to be healed. So many of these stories seemed to conflict with the stories that the Shaman was telling the tribe about spirits.

Tregor was careful to tell his children not to tell any other children the stories they were learning from Toyuk, that they would be punished if the Shaman Rohue found out.

In the telling of the stories each night Toyuk learned how to listen closely to the Holy Spirit as He interpreted the stories into Toyuk's language. Toyuk was learning how to listen skillfully, both to the Holy Spirit and to others. The Holy Spirit was teaching Toyuk about His Fruit and how He moved through people with His power. Toyuk taking the role of storyteller to the family had helped Toyuk sort through many concepts he had been pondering, especially as he listened to the Holy Spirit interpret the stories for the family. It was a great spiritual maturing time for Toyuk.

It was after a dinner one night and Toyuk was sitting in front of his entrance when Nea came and sat down next to him.

"Do you think Jesus would have healed me? I wish I could have been there with Jesus."

Toyuk smiled. He knew his stories were impacting Tregor's family. "Well, Nea, Jesus is alive now. And He still heals today." Toyuk could tell the Holy Spirit was directing his speech and speaking through him. That fact that Jesus healed today made Toyuk surprised at what the Holy Spirit was saying through him.

"What do you mean?" Nea was wide eyed. "Do you mean He could show up and heal me now?!"

Toyuk paused, waiting for the Holy Spirit's response.

"Well... Nea, He actually could come in person and heal you now. He is after all One with the Great Spirit; nothing is impossible for Him. But He now usually asks one of His own who is filled with His Holy Spirit to follow His instructions and pray for people to be healed. There were men called Peter and Paul that Jesus worked through that many were healed by Jesus through the power of the Holy Spirit."

Nea sat quietly thinking about what Toyuk had just told her. "You met Jesus, maybe you could pray for me?" Nea spoke softly.

"Nea, why don't we pray together to Jesus and the Great Spirit. Thank the Great Spirit for His Son Jesus, that He died for your mistakes and wrongs against the Great Spirit, and that you want Him to live inside of you."

"I want to, Toyuk, but I don't know exactly what to say."

"Just speak to Him the way you speak to me. The Great Spirit loves you. He actually is the one who formed you in Nayee's belly. Just speak to Him like you would to a good friend."

Nea was quiet for a time. Then she slowly began to talk to the Great Spirit. "Great Spirit, I really don't know what to say or how to talk to you, but I believe Toyuk. I believe the story of Your Son Jesus and what He did for me. Great Spirit, Jesus... would you please heal me?"

"That was perfect, Nea." Toyuk then began to pray. "Father in Heaven, we know You are our Creator. You can do all things. I know You love Nea. I, too, ask that You heal Nea, heal her heart, heal her hurt, and heal her leg. In the name of Jesus, my friend, Your Son, I ask You." Toyuk then opened his eyes and saw Nea was crying. "Are you okay?"

"I felt something like I've never felt before, like waves of warmth passing through my entire body, it's almost too much. It feels like warm love and like warm oil." Nea was talking quietly through her tears.

Toyuk looked at Nea's leg and nothing had changed.

Trust me, came the reply from the Holy Spirit in his mind.

"Thank you, Toyuk." Nea got up and slipped into the dwelling.

Toyuk's heart was so impacted by what had just happened. He was trying hard to figure out what he was feeling and what He should do. He was full of mixed emotions.

Trust me. These words of the Holy Spirit were echoing in his mind.

The next morning early at dawn just before sunrise Toyuk and the entire family were awakened by screaming. Nea's screaming.

Toyuk stuck his head through the opening. What he saw was amazing.

Nea was jumping, spinning, hopping, screaming, and laughing all at the same time. The entire family was watching Nea with wide eyes. Nea's leg showed no signs of any kind of wound, or deformity, or problems, and obviously was working marvelously. Soon the other children were dancing and jumping with her. Tregor was hugging Nayee. Nayee was crying loudly with joy!

Toyuk quickly got up and dressed and moved into the main dwelling as fast as he could. By then the entire family was hugging and dancing.

When they saw Toyuk, they stopped. Tregor and Nayee asked Toyuk, "What did you do?"

"I only prayed to the Great Spirit in agreement with what Nea prayed to Him. Nea accepted Jesus as the Great Spirit's Son and asked Him to heal her."

"And obviously He did!!" Nea almost shouted. That led to another round of dancing but this time Toyuk joined in. After a time of joyful celebration, the family had plopped down and were breathing heavily and laughing.

Tregor then started talking and everyone went silent, except he wasn't talking to them. "Great Spirit, Jesus, I thank you for healing my daughter. I recognize now You are the Great Spirit our Creator. I accept Jesus is Your Son. Please forgive me for being selfish and thinking more about myself than others. Forgive me, Great Spirit, for treating Toyuk badly before. Thank You for bringing Toyuk back and giving me this opportunity to learn from him about You."

Tregor stopped and Nayee could see Tregor was so emotional he couldn't speak any further. Nayee grabbed Tregor and hugged him fiercely. Then Toyuk grabbed both Tregor and Nayee and hugged them. Then Nea and the children came and joined the hug.

The time afterward led to each family member talking to the Great Spirit and accepting and thanking His Son Jesus. Nayee had never felt this happy. Nea was now always swaying and dancing; she couldn't stop moving. That morning was filled with happy tears from everyone.

Tregor had a new bounce to his step that day. He walked with purpose and wore a smile that was unusual for him. Nayee was constantly humming. Nea was actually seen, as she almost never ventured out much before, but now was seen at the river and outside around their dwelling—walking normally, and what looked like dancing.

Ona was the first to see a huge difference in the Tregor family. She quickly walked over and questioned Nayee.

"What has happened? The family of Tregor has changed... for the better!"

Just then Nayee had an experience she hadn't encountered before—a Voice spoke in her mind and gave her this thought: *Invite Ona and Miccoon for dinner and then tell them what happened inside your dwelling.*

"Ona, we would be honored if Miccoon and yourself would join us for dinner tonight."

"Nayee, that would be wonderful, I'll bring honey cakes." Ona was beaming with a huge smile.

"Aren't you going to ask Miccoon first?" Nayee was a little surprised Ona agreed so quickly.

"Miccoon had already suggested we invite your entire family over for dinner. I'm sure he will come."

"After dinner Tregor and I will tell you what has happened to us. And I'm sure everyone one will be thrilled to enjoy your honey cakes. Toyuk has been sharing the ones he got from Miccoon from you with the children. Gnut will be so happy you'll be bringing more."

Ona walked away amazed at the change she saw in Nayee—it was like she wasn't even the same person. She was excited to get ready for the shared dinner that night. She couldn't wait to tell Miccoon.

Toyuk had slipped away after that morning celebration and felt drawn high up into the mountains. The whole way his heart couldn't stop praising and thanking the Great Spirit, Jesus, and the Holy Spirit. The air seemed especially sweet, clear, and glorious. Toyuk felt the strength of the Holy Spirit flowing through him. On the bank of a high Sierra crystal clear lake, he sat down in soft grass and then just lay there... in joy. He wasn't hungry, or tired, or thirsty. He felt like he was experiencing the Kingdom of the Great Spirit, where there is no lack.

That evening around the Tregor family cooking fire sat the family, Miccoon and Ona, and Toyuk. Ona and Miccoon watched with amazement how much joy was being shared during the meal. The conversation and laughter were so easy. After dinner Tregor invited Miccoon and Ona into their dwelling. It was a bit cramped and tight, but no one seemed to mind.

Tregor asked Toyuk to share what had happened the previous evening. Toyuk explained how Nea and he prayed to the Great Spirit and His Son Jesus to heal Nea.

Just after that story, Tregor jumped in telling Miccoon and Ona of the dancing celebration that had happened that morning. Miccoon and Ona looked at Tregor wondering who this man was now, he was so filled with joy and humble and thankful. Nayee almost cut Tregor off and told of his prayer and her prayer, and the family's acceptance of Jesus the Son of the Great Spirit.

"So that's what has happened to the Tregor family," Nea pronounced.

"We now serve the Great Spirit and His Son Jesus," Tregor quickly confirmed.

"Is this the Jesus you've mentioned to me, Toyuk?" Ona was looking at Toyuk with a knowing smile.

"Yes, Ona, He is the One I met in the Petersons' barn. He is the One who told me to learn of Him in this…" Toyuk held up his Bible. "It's the book the Great Spirit allowed me to bring with me back to this time."

Everyone in the family had wondered about the strange skin Toyuk would often look at while telling his stories.

"We too will serve the Great Spirit and His Son Jesus," Miccoon stated clearly. "I have long recognized the touch of the Great Spirit on Toyuk. He speaks truth."

"Yes, Miccoon is right." Ona said plainly, nodding with a serious look on her face. "I praise the Great Spirit for giving me such a wise husband and warrior. I agree too and will serve the Great Spirit and His Son Jesus."

A time of speaking to the Great Spirit and Jesus was spent by each family member down to the youngest child. Then Ona and Miccoon spoke their own words to the Great Spirit. Tears were flowing. Everyone was hugging. The youngest Tregor family child ended up in Miccoon's lap and another was hanging onto Ona.

"You are officially our adopted parents, elders, and family. We love you, Miccoon and Ona." Tregor made the announcement, with all of the rest of his family agreeing wildly.

"Tregor, you've changed." Miccoon was speaking what he was thinking.

"Yes I have, Miccoon. I can actually feel the Great Spirit now inside me, it's hard to explain."

"That's the Holy Spirit, Tregor," Toyuk said quietly.

"The Holy Spirit will speak to you in your head. You will learn to recognize His Voice in your mind," Toyuk quietly shared.

"Wait, the Holy Spirit—is He the same as the Great Spirit?" Nayee was genuinely asking Toyuk.

"Yes, Nayee. The Great Spirit is Three but also One, which is still a mystery to me, but the Holy Spirit is teaching me and helping me know all the different sides to the Great Spirit."

"So He speaks in your mind, you hear Him like thoughts?" Nayee was really focused now, and everyone was also listening intently.

"Yes, Nayee. But there are ways other spirits, actual enemies of the Great Spirit, can also put thoughts into your mind, so you will have to learn when it is Him, when it yourself, and when it is a spirit that wants harm to come to you. I'm still learning, Nayee, but I am getting better at knowing Who is speaking in my thoughts." Toyuk now had everyone looking at him.

"I think it was this Holy Spirit who spoke in my head today to invite Ona and Miccoon to dinner," Nayee said, beginning to realize.

Everyone agreed that having Miccoon and Ona over for dinner was a great and right thing.

"I agree, Nayee. That sounds very much like the Holy Spirit to me." Toyuk held up his Bible.

"I have His story here and it helps me learn what He would say and what He would do, so that I can better understand where my thoughts could be coming from. It might take me my entire life, but I'm determined to put this Bible into our language, so that all of you can have this same knowledge I have, so that we can know what it is He speaks to us intimately in our minds and hearts. This will confirm His words to us."

"I've been hearing from Him for a while now, Toyuk. I accepted Jesus as the Great Spirit's Son when you shared your experience with me that you had in the other time," Ona said quietly with a smile.

"So that's why you've been extra happy lately?" Miccoon asked Ona looking at her with a smile.

"I guess so," Ona replied. Toyuk was grinning from ear to ear, he couldn't stop smiling.

"Well, I guess you need to be a part of our family story time every night from now on," Tregor suggested strongly. Tregor was feeling so different. Nayee was looking at him in amazement.

"Miccoon and I will ask the Great Spirit what we should do now," Ona said quietly. "But your offer is truly honoring to us. My heart says yes, but I think now as servants of the Great Spirit we need to be asking Him what we should be doing.... everyday." Ona was truly emotional now.

"Ona is correct, I agree with her. We do need to check with the Great Spirit in everything we do.

At least that's what I'm learning." Toyuk was quick to reply to Ona's suggestion.

Miccoon and Ona began to get up, and all the hugging began all over again. Goodbyes and thanks were said by everyone. The youngest child didn't want to let go of Miccoon. He picked her up and held her close and whispered in her ear. "I will come back and take you fishing. Would you like that?"

She hugged him all the more.

Miccoon put her down and walked out of the dwelling with Ona.

15

———— ◆ ————

CONFRONTATION AND ACCEPTANCE

The next days were so filled with joy. Miccoon and Ona had been over at the Tregor family dwelling almost every night. If they missed, the younger Tregor children would be running over to see why they hadn't come, which usually meant they missed Ona's honey corn cakes.

Miccoon was so happy to play grandfather to them.

Nea was feeling bolder and more confident. She was even resuming the usual outside chores, like being at the river, and joining Nayee in the vegetable area, with the other women. She no longer held her head down when she walked, and now actually looked at other women in the eyes and greeted them with a smile. She didn't care how short her hair was, and it was growing back fairly fast.

Toyuk, Tregor, and Miccoon were often now seen together going off hunting, or fishing, and leaving the village area. Miccoon gave his knowledge of the river and different types of fish and where to find them. Tregor gave his knowledge of the forest and animal ways and habitats, as well as his bow aiming tips and how to have a clean and fast kill. Toyuk usually talked about what the Great Spirit was teaching him out of the Bible. Together amongst the three, there was a growing respect and admiration of the gifts and skills each man had. They began to realize they were better as a group than when they were alone and began to seek one another out when they had the chance.

The tribe had also seen the changes in this little group that was forming. Rohue was seen more and more visiting the Chief's dwelling. Kinar and Rohue were often seen talking quietly together and others wondered what they were planning. The biggest topic and gossip of the tribe revolved around Nea. Everyone saw the huge, obvious change in her. Her leg was perfectly normal now and Nea could be seen skipping and running from place to place. Of course, Rohue wanted to use the situation for his benefit. Kinar made an announcement and called a tribal wide meeting in three nights. People wondered why the delay, so that only spurred more gossip.

The new group could not have cared less about the coming big tribal meeting. They were enjoying their own tribal meeting every night. But when the night came, they joined around the village fire to listen to what Kinar had to say.

Rohue was in full spirit costume, and began his usual dance and chants to the spirits at the beginning of the meeting. He suddenly stopped and dramatically looked all around at the tribe members.

"The spirits have blessed our tribe. Our offerings have been accepted! There is one here who has received their power." The tribe hushed, waiting for the next thing Rohue would say. Rohue walked around with his arm in the air as he moved closer and closer to tribe members. He stopped just before Nea and his arm pointed at her. "You have been blessed by the offerings I have given to the spirits; you have received their blessing and the spirits healed your leg!"

Rohue then moved away, and members of the tribe let out yells, and cries of thanks to the spirits.

Toyuk and his group were looking extremely stern during this time. They did not have joy on their faces.

Nea then did something no one expected. She got up and started shouting... at Rohue. When the tribe saw and heard Nea shouting at Rohue they stopped and got quiet.

"The spirits DID NOT HEAL MY LEG! JESUS DID!!! Your offerings DID NOTHING! My father and family paid you too much—NOTHING you did helped me." Nea was obviously angry.

Rohue stood still. The tribe stood still. It seemed like no one was breathing. The silence was deafening.

"The Great Spirit's Son Jesus healed my leg when I asked Him. You did nothing," Nea said defiantly.

"Child, what do you know about the spirits and their ways?" Rohue was slowly walking towards Nea and speaking with scorn, and a twisted angry face.

Just then Toyuk stood up and walked to Nea and stood next to her. "Nea may not know spirits like you, Rohue, but she does know the Son of the Great Spirit, as He now lives within her," Toyuk spoke directly and firmly to Rohue.

Rohue stopped walking towards them. "What do you know... 'boy'?" Rohue almost spat the words out.

"What I know, Rohue, is you manipulate people, so you look big and powerful. You don't really know the Great Spirit... only of Him. And that what you think you know about Him is... wrong." There were gasps heard throughout the tribe. "The spirits you deal with want to harm us more than help us. Those are the spirits you know. The Great Spirit is WHO I know, and His Son Jesus, and His Holy Spirit."

"Well, ...boy... then we'll just need to test this knowledge of yours. You think yourself so high and mighty now with your little group. Yes, everyone here sees you," Rohue said with acid on his tongue.

Every one of the tribe members were riveted to their spots. They were sure a showdown was coming.

Tregor had gotten up and tried to lead Nea back to the family spot, but Nea resisted until Ona came and held her arm and gently and convinced her to walk back. That left Toyuk still standing, —alone—facing Rohue.

"I'm not going to fight you, Rohue. But I won't allow you or the spirits to take credit for something they and you did not do." Toyuk was calm and direct.

"You think you know the spirits better than me?" Rohue asked in a mocking tone.

"No. I think I know the Great Spirit better than you. The Great Spirit created everything we know, even those spirits you think you know," Toyuk said calmly.

Just then the Holy Spirit spoke in Toyuk's mind. *"Tell him you'll meet him here at the same time in three nights with the entire tribe to witness who has the knowledge of the spirits."*

Rohue stood defiantly and with a snarl on his face.

Toyuk continued. "Rohue... I will answer everyone's questions here about the Great Spirit... in three nights from now in front of the entire tribe... you and I will face off with our knowledge of the spirits," Toyuk spoke forcefully.

"Accepted... boy." With that, Rohue spun on his heels and stormed out of the circle with his animal skins flapping and went straight to his dwelling.

"Three nights from now," Kinar stated loudly and walked away.

The tribe began to break up and go back to their dwellings. Toyuk walked back to the group.

Tregor put his arm around Toyuk and asked quietly, "What are you going to do?"

"I don't know, Tregor. I just said what the Holy Spirit told me to say at that moment. I'm not sure what He has planned." Toyuk was feeling like he was slowing down from a big adrenaline rush and feeling exhausted.

That night Tregor, Nayee, Ona, and Miccoon all had very vivid dreams. The dreams were detailed and full of color. In the morning Ona headed to the Tregor dwelling to talk to Toyuk. Nayee saw Ona coming towards her and called out to her.

"Ona, I need to talk to you right now." Nayee was very insistent.

"Last night I had a very vivid dream, it seemed like it was happening in real life." Nayee was watching Ona's face.

Ona obviously was extremely interested in everything Nayee was telling her. "Stop, Nayee. Don't tell me anymore. I too had a dream last night, and it also seemed very real. Let's go inside and get Tregor and Toyuk to listen to our dreams."

Nayee saw Tregor and Toyuk coming back from the river and waved them over. When they were all inside the dwelling, Ona started explaining that both Nayee and herself had very vivid dreams last night. Tregor tilted his head and became very interested, because he too had had a vivid dream but hadn't disclosed it to anyone. He wasn't sure how to explain it.

Ona began, "In my dream I was walking with our group, and we were all going north. Everyone was just talking like normal, but we had all of our belongings with us, like we were all moving to a new area."

Nayee jumped in as Ona took a breath, "...and we were going north of the sacred valley, to find an area with a lake and good river."

Ona just stared at Nayee in great surprise.

Tregor then said, "Toyuk and I took turns leading the way. The children were doing well."

Now both Ona and Nayee were staring at Tregor.

"It seems to me that the Great Spirit has been busy giving you all the same dream." Toyuk smiled.

"What does this mean Toyuk?" Ona asked.

"I've learned the hard way that all the correct interpretations of dreams come from the Holy Spirit. All of you must now seek Him and ask Him questions as to what the dream means, and what you should be doing. Not for anyone else but for yourself and what exactly He wants you to do. I've certainly made many mistakes trying to figure out dreams on my own." They were all listening intently to Toyuk and nodding as he was explaining. "I suggest that all of you seek the Holy Spirit today and ask Him about the dream you had. Tonight, we all can share what we heard from Him."

"That sounds good, Toyuk." Tregor was already standing up.

Toyuk continued, "I've never encountered several people having the same dream in one night, but I think it would be good if we didn't discuss them any further with each other until all of us personally have gotten instructions from the Holy Spirit as to what each of us are to do. That way we get His view rather than someone else's interpretation." Toyuk was standing up and Nayee and Ona then got up as well.

"Tonight should be an interesting time," Ona said as she hugged Nayee.

Ona headed back to her dwelling. Miccoon was sitting out front working on making arrows. Tregor and Toyuk headed out and began walking north carrying their bows.

"So why were you in such a big rush this morning?" Miccoon asked, looking up at Ona.

"I had a dream last night and I went to visit Toyuk to tell him the dream, but I found out that Tregor, and Nayee had the very same dream. We're all going to discuss together tonight what we hear from the Holy Spirit and what His instructions are for each of us." Ona was now sitting down next to Miccoon.

"I, too, had a dream. It was the most vivid colorful dream I have ever had."

"We were walking north, all of us..." Ona had not waited to listen any further about Miccoon's dream.

"No." Miccoon interrupted Ona and paused, he waited for her to be still and quiet.

Ona was surprised—she thought that Miccoon had also been given the same dream.

"In my dream I was in a different world or land. The land of our Chief Jesus, where He now lives. The mountains were bigger than any I have ever seen. The grass, flowers, trees, and even the rocks had all their own... sound. Even the water was... wetter and had a... much richer, wider sound than any river I have known. So much of this is hard for me to describe. Everything seemed SO alive. There was a huge village in the distance, and it gave off so many beautiful colors. There were so many things there I don't know how to explain, things I saw, heard, felt... so many languages and sounds. But it was the beings there, and the people... they were the same but... more... some you could kind of see through. It was more than I could almost take in, but I wasn't scared at all, I didn't want the dream to end." Miccoon was starting and stopping as he was trying to describe what he had experienced in his dream. He searched for words to describe things, but he had no experiential reference or words to explain them.

Ona was silent waiting to see if Miccoon needed any more time. When he stayed silent, she was in awe of how she could see Miccoon's dream had affected him and reverently relayed Toyuk's advice of seeking the Holy Spirit with any questions and interpretations He would give Miccoon.

"I guess Toyuk should know. He's lived through some of his dreams. I will take some time and go seek the Holy Spirit on my dream." Miccoon got up, put the arrows in their dwelling, and walked north while Ona set about thinking about what she will prepare special for this evening's dinner.

That night's dinner the children seemed to feel like the adults were rushing through the meal. Then they were told to go play, but if they stayed to listen that they would have to remain silent while everyone else talked. The children all chose to listen. Nea gathered them in the far back corner and the three of them sat on soft fur skins.

As they all sat in the dwelling, the light was dim, but everyone could see well enough. Everyone decided that Ona, then Nayee, then Tregor would tell their dreams and what the Holy Spirit had told them and instructed them to do.

Ona told her dream and that she said the Holy Spirit was telling her to get ready for a trip. She said the Holy Spirit showed her specifically what she should take and what she had to give away.

Nayee talked about how the Holy Spirit warned her that she would have difficulty on the trip, and that she needed to learn to trust Him more. Nayee said the last part very quietly. Ona reached out and put her hand on Nayee's shoulder.

Tregor had difficulty sharing. He shared that he could not reveal everything the Holy Spirit had told him, and that he had many things to do in the next three days. But what he did share was the Holy Spirit said there were things he needed to make right with certain members of the greater tribe. Everyone could tell that Tregor was taking these things very seriously.

Then Ona gently prodded Miccoon to tell everyone his dream, and anything the Holy Spirit would allow him to share. Miccoon took his time and tried his best to relay some of his dream. It was difficult for Miccoon because the words didn't come easily. At the end he shared that the Holy Spirit said that He was preparing Miccoon for a trip as well. And that more of his instructions from the Holy Spirit would come at a later time. Miccoon shared he wasn't used to all of this dreaming and talking with the Great Spirit kind of experience, that it was Ona's realm, not his.

Everyone was so still while Miccoon talked and amazed at the dream that was given to Miccoon.

It obviously was very different from the one the Great Spirit had given to the others. Everyone wanted Miccoon to describe more of his dream but knew he had great difficulty sharing what he did, so they just pondered what was shared hoping that at a later time they might be able to ask Miccoon questions about it.

Toyuk then began to share. "Well it looks like we all have a lot to do in the next three days. Let's all keep ourselves focused on the Holy Spirit as much as possible. It looks like the Great Spirit will be taking us all on a trip. I'm not sure if that trip will begin in three days, or later. But obviously we all have something coming up. I know I have a lot of questions for the Holy Spirit that I want to know about the meeting coming up. Whether He will tell me, I'm not sure. It seems He likes to wait to the very last moment. I will have to stay focused on Him and not let any distractions get in my way. I want you all to know how much I'm glad I get to have this adventure with each one of you. You are my family and I love each of you."

There were hugs all around, and children asked if they then could speak. Nayee said yes. The children quickly asked if Toyuk could tell a story before they had to sleep. Of course, Toyuk agreed.

Toyuk then grabbed Ona in a hug and whispered in her ear, "I miss my mom." Ona squeezed Toyuk tight.

Miccoon and Ona left for the evening after Miccoon gave a hug to his adoptive granddaughter who always needed a hug.

16

STORY AND CHALLENGE

The next tribe meeting time was fast approaching, and the group was busy trying to be ready and follow the instructions they thought they were receiving from the Holy Spirit. They would often check with Toyuk for him to tell them what the Great Spirit's teaching in the skin, or Bible, about something they felt like the Holy Spirit was telling them to do. Toyuk would then ask the Holy Spirit for the story or situation in the scriptures that could help address the instructions they felt they were receiving.

Toyuk was definitely feeling the need to put the scriptures into his language, so that everyone could just read for themselves the confirmation in the Word. It then dawned on him that he also would need to teach most of them how to read, and that there were so many concepts and words in the Bible his own language didn't convey or even have. The task ahead of Toyuk was long. He didn't mind helping those he loved, but he also knew the danger of becoming their mediator between them and the Great Spirit. He certainly didn't want to become another... Rohue.

In the early afternoon before the meeting the Holy Spirit gave Toyuk his first instruction about the meeting.

Put on the clothes you had when you arrived back to your village.

Toyuk wondered why.

Because you are still an outcast in their eyes and your clothing will stand out to them that you are different, came the quick response to his thoughts.

Even though Toyuk didn't want to continue to be an outcast he obeyed and went to get the bundle of his old clothes. He put them all on with the shoes.

Nayee took one look at Toyuk and the dirty clothes he had on and went quickly over to him. "Those skins need to be washed. Leto dragged you through the forest in those. Take them off and

I will quickly wash them for you."

Toyuk humbly complied and changed back into his regular skins and handed the clothes to Nayee. Nea had seen Nayee's and Toyuk's conversation and came to offer help to Nayee to get Toyuk's clothes washed.

"Together it will go much quicker," Nea said to Nayee.

In the late afternoon his clothes had dried and Toyuk put them on again.

"You certainly don't look like one of us." Nea commented.

"I guess that's the point of why the Holy Spirit told me to change into them." Toyuk then lowered his voice and spoke softly to Nea. "I'm actually nervous about tonight. I don't know how it will go. I don't want to put any of you in danger, especially you, Nea."

"We trust you Toyuk. We know the Great Spirit is with you and us," Nea said gently and quietly and gave Toyuk a hug.

The tribe had gathered and there was anticipation as to what Kinar and Rohue would do with the growing division happening in the tribe.

Kinar stood and spoke to the tribe. "Tonight, we will listen to Rohue and his knowledge of the spirits. We will also hear from the man who calls himself Toyuk who has challenged the understanding we all have of the spirits that have guided us from our ancestors. Since we all know how the spirits work, we will allow the outsider to now speak."

Toyuk stepped forward one pace from the circle. "It seems my entire life has been leading to this moment. All of you knew me as a boy, son of Tonuw and Shushe. Many of you know my father was killed defending this tribe. I was like every other boy in this tribe who couldn't wait for the day that we would be allowed to go through the initiation challenge. We worked hard to be ready, taught by our wise elders to learn our ways, like Miccoon and Tregor." Toyuk paused and began to speak in a humble tone. "Growing up from a very young age I was given very disturbing dreams. I woke up many a time with my heart racing and sweating from the encounters happening to me in those dreams. I struggled to understand why I was having these dreams. Then, on the last day of the initiation, I found out why I was having those dreams. First with an encounter with the Great White Buck, and then with an encounter with the Son of the Great Spirit."

Toyuk paused again and looked up at the sky, and then continued. "Something happened to me that I still can't fully explain. The Great Spirit took me to the time of the dreams I had been having. I saw things I did things I will not be able to explain to you today, for there is nothing like it here in this time. If I tried, the story would be too hard to believe, because you've never seen anything like it. But there in that time and place I saw the Great White Buck again who disappeared before my eyes, and then a blinding light forced me to the ground. He called Himself the Son of the Great Spirit, and his name was… Jesus. I was told to learn of Him. Then He blew on me and I was filled with His Spirit. His Voice now speaks to me in my mind. I spent thirty-six moons in that place of my dreams learning and growing. I learned of the Great Spirit, His Son, and another side to the Great Spirit. He is the Creator of all things. Jesus calls Him Father, yet He is One with Him, as is the Great Spirit. Three in One, a mystery I still cannot completely understand. The Creator created all things. The lights in the heavens, every spirit, animal, and land. The rivers, mountains, and great waters." Toyuk paused again and looked at everyone sitting in the circle.

Toyuk was now using his story voice. "Before the Creator made this land, there was a war in His creation. A powerful, beautiful spirit decided to rebel against the Creator; he wanted to take the place of the Creator. The spirit led one third of the spirits to rebel against their Maker. Then the Creator made this land and animals, and the first man and woman and put them into a beautiful forest, where everything was easy to have. Then the spirit who was against the Great Spirit came to deceive the man and the woman. The man and woman listened to that powerful, persuasive spirit and went against what the Great Spirit had told them to do. Because of their disobedience, the Great Spirit cast them out of that forest and cut them off from being able to communicate directly with Him. But the Great Spirit still loved us, because we are His children. So, He provided a way that we might gain our relationship back with Him. He allowed a woman to bear His Son. His name was Jesus and He taught about His Father to the people. But the spirits who are against the Great Spirit didn't like Jesus; they wanted to kill Him. So, they told lies to people so that they would hate Him, too, and they killed Him by nailing Him to a tree. The Son said He died so that all the mistakes we have made against the Great Spirit could be forgiven, that He would pay our complete debt. The evil spirits thought they had won. But three days later Jesus rose from death and walked among His tribe again. Jesus then rose into the heavens to be with His Father telling His Tribe He would send the Great Spirit to live inside them, so that they would know what the Great Spirit wants them to do and to have great joy." Toyuk stopped and sighed. He began quietly making everyone listen closely to his words.

"Someday when my body dies, my spirit will be taken by His great warriors to live with Jesus and His Father with the Great Spirit in their land in the heavens, and there I will be given a new body, one that cannot die. I have been watching, learning, and listening. I have thought long about our traditions, history, and stories. I have seen the Great Spirit in many things around us; He has provided many great things for us to know Him better. But we also have been attacked and hurt by the spirits that are enemies of the Great Spirit. We cannot always tell what spirit is good or bad. This is why we have our Shaman. He is to teach us the spirits' ways—what the spirits require of us. I have come to learn that these spirits need to be tested. If the spirit acknowledges the Great Spirit's Son Jesus then they are on His side, if they do not, they are the spirits who rebelled against the Great Spirit and hate all of us." Toyuk paused for effect and looked directly at Rohue.

"The Great Spirit and His Son Jesus is the one whom Nea prayed to for her leg to be healed.

At night the Great Spirit did a big work in Nea and in the morning her leg was healed and back to normal. The spirits who hate the Great Spirit wanted to keep Nea crippled; they wanted her dead.

The Great Spirit wants us to learn of Him and talk with Him, all of us … not just the Shaman."

This brought the first reaction in the tribe, and the people were surprised to hear this, and Rohue stood up.

"I do not know of any son of the Great Spirit. You obviously don't know much about the spirits.

You spin stories to lead us away from our traditions so that you will gain power. Prove to us that what you say is true." Rohue was calm but it was obvious he was not happy with the story Toyuk just told.

Toyuk spoke in his mind, *"What would you like me to do?"*

The response was immediate. *"Set a target at two hundred paces away with no trees between."*

"I've been told by the Great Spirit to set a target two hundred paces away with no trees in the way," Toyuk stated.

The crowd wondered what would happen next, because no one can hit a target in the dark which they cannot see.

Kinar picked up the skin of a wolf and nodded to a warrior. That warrior with Toyuk at his side walked out into the forest, with Toyuk watching the tribal fire while also counting his steps. At the distance they found a tree and hung the skin from a branch. As they got back Toyuk then spoke to Rohue.

"The spirits guide us... yes? Then choose a warrior and we will allow the spirits to guide our chosen warriors in hitting the target with an arrow."

Rohue looked concerned, he couldn't even see the target. The target was really far away. "How will we know if one hits the target?"

"Let warriors be set where they can see the wolf skin," Toyuk replied.

Kinar waved and three warriors ran to position themselves behind trees but could still see the wolf skin. "Rohue... choose your warrior."

"I choose Kinar, our best greatest warrior and marksman." Proudly Rohue pointed at Kinar.

"I suggest for Kinar's sake that we provide a light so that Kinar can see the target in the distance.

Let us say hitting the head of the wolf is the goal," Toyuk suggested.

Kinar called back the warriors and gave them instructions. They took some branches and lit them on fire, then went and cleared the ground before the tree and set the branches before the skin.

There in the great distance was the wolf skin dimly lit against the dark, an almost impossible target.

Kinar then stepped up and took aim. Kinar let an arrow go. Then a warrior's yell could be heard in the distance.

The warrior came back with a report that Kinar actually had hit the wolf skin, but at the very bottom. The tribe warriors let out large war cries and yells in celebration. The people were amazed at their Chief.

"The spirits favor our Chief with power!" Rohue stated loudly.

Toyuk had gone back to sit with Tregor and family while watching Kinar shoot. After the shot, Toyuk got up and walked to the center. Everyone was expecting him to pick up a bow to take a shot. What happened next was not expected.

"Nea, would you please come here?" Toyuk gently asked and motioned for Nea to join him. "Kinar, please have your warriors snuff out the branches so the target will be dark." Then Toyuk left Nea standing there and went to get his bow, arrows, and a small animal skin from Ona.

When he returned, he tied the animal skin around Nea's head so she couldn't see. He then put the bow into Nea's hands with an arrow notched and ready to go.

"Toyuk, I can't do this," Nea whispered loudly.

"Exactly. Nea, listen to the Great Spirit, do what He tells you to do. The battle is His, not ours. We are just to play our part."

Toyuk led Nea to the far edge of the circle. People began to snicker and laugh. It seemed funny because no one could do what Toyuk was setting up Nea to do. No one even knew if Nea could shoot a bow, no one had seen her try before. Then Toyuk did another thing that no one expected. He began to turn Nea around. Three times Toyuk spun Nea around. Then he told her to shoot.

Nea steadied herself. She drew the bow back aimed at what seemed to be way right of the target, raised the bow high, and let go of the arrow. Just then a wind could be heard at the top of the trees, and a war cry was heard. The warrior brought back the wolf skin with an arrow through the head.

People were stunned. Some were angry. Kinar looked mad. Others were turning and talking and pointing. The Tregor family and Miccoon and Ona were smiling.

Rohue raised his arms and the people quieted down. "Toyuk, this only proves what I said before. The spirits have blessed Nea, they accepted my offerings to them. This helps me more than you."

Toyuk wasn't quite sure what to say. He was asking for the response he was supposed to give, but he got instructions from the Holy Spirit instead. "Kinar, allow me to put the skin back on the branch."

"I will not shoot again," Kinar said defiantly.

"You won't, someone else will."

Toyuk went with the three warriors and set the wolf skin on the branch and came back to the circle, leaving the three warriors to watch the target. Toyuk then went and got Ona. Ona was surprised, but willing after what she just saw happened with Nea. Toyuk tied the animal skin around Ona's head.

"I will not spin Ona, as I respect her, and she is my elder."

Everyone including Miccoon knew Ona would never be able to hit the target without the Great Spirit's help. She wasn't strong enough. Everyone in the tribe knew that as well. Rohue's smile was like a cat before the pounce.

Toyuk led Ona to the edge of the circle. "I'll give you the same instructions I gave Nea. Do only what the Great Spirit tells you to do. The battle is His, we just do our part. Shoot the arrow when you're ready."

Toyuk stepped back from Ona so no one could say he had helped her. The silence was loud as everyone waited for Ona to try to pull the bow back. It was amazing enough that Nea had done it, but Ona? Everyone knew this was impossible.

Ona tried to pull the bow back but could only barely move the string. Everyone waited. Then all of a sudden, Ona pulled the bow string all the way back and launched the arrow, and again the wind could be heard in the trees.

War cries could be heard, and the warriors brought back the wolf skin with an arrow in the head.

When the warriors got back there was no celebration, no cries, no yells, just... silence. No one could believe what had just happened. No one knew... how. Except for Tregor, Nayee, Nea, Miccoon, and Toyuk, who were equally amazed... but they knew the Source of the miracle. Ona had taken off the animal skin and gone to sit down next to Miccoon.

"How were you able to pull that bow back?" Miccoon quietly asked Ona.

"I talked to the Great Spirit in my head. I heard Him tell me to think of Him and trust Him. Then He told me, 'Now!' loudly in my head, and the bow just seemed easy to pull back." Ona half smiled with a shrug of her shoulders.

Toyuk then faced Rohue.

"The Great Spirit guides us, as He give us strength for the impossible task at hand, as well as our effort, as in this example ... Ona's arrow. Nea used that same Great Spirit, not the spirits you say helped her."

Toyuk turned and walked back to the Tregor family who were already getting up to leave.

Rohue was left standing alone as everyone got up to go back.

17

— • —

UNEXPECTED EVENTS

The next morning everything seemed to be back to normal, as the breakfast fires were going, the regular crowd was cleaning at the river. Boys were still diving off the rock. Life was just going on as it always had. Except—members of the tribe were discretely coming to Tregor, Nayee, Miccoon, and Ona and asking them questions about the events of the previous night and about the Great Spirit. Conversations were being held out of direct sight of others. Even some of the younger newly married women were carefully approaching Nea and asking her questions.

This was a new thing to Nea since her accident. Before the accident, Nea was seen as one of the popular desired ones, but after the accident no one wanted to associate with her. Now, after her healing and display at the previous night's event, the young women were curious to understand this confidence that was so evident now in Nea. Nea was sharing about how the Great Spirit and Jesus had healed her leg and her soul, and was taking away the darkness in her heart and replacing it with joy.

Tregor and Toyuk had set out early before sunrise on a hunt. Tregor was learning more about how the Great Spirit was dwelling within him by the instructions and direction the Holy Spirit was giving him. Toyuk listened and often prayed asking for words on how to respond to all that Tregor was sharing. Their relationship was growing, and Toyuk often found himself asking Tregor about his father and what he was like. Toyuk still was seeking for elder male mentor examples because of the missing father relationship in his life. Toyuk pondered these things, as well as listened intently to the Holy Spirit on these personal issues that surrounded his heart. Miccoon had always seemed to fill that grandfather role in Toyuk's life, and Toyuk loved him greatly. And now Tregor was filling another type of role in his life, one that he hadn't ever had before. Sure, there was Erik Peterson but Tregor was now much closer to understanding, learning, and growing in and with the Holy Spirit. Plus, Tregor was asking Toyuk questions and was engaging him in a relationship more than Erik had done while Toyuk lived in that time. Tregor and Toyuk were spending a lot of time together.

When Tregor and Toyuk were returning to the village with deer meat, they could tell there was a great commotion going on. Nayee ran to Tregor and Toyuk, telling them that Miccoon had been in an accident. Tregor and Toyuk dropped off the meat at the dwelling and ran to Miccoon's and Ona's dwelling. Ona had already told Rohue to get out, which had also caused a stir among the village. Tregor and Toyuk found Miccoon lying still in their dwelling. He seemed to be breathing heavy and his eyes were closed. They asked Ona what had happened. Ona began telling the story in a hushed voice.

"He was just going to his regular fishing spot when a branch from a large tree fell on top of him. He was crushed by the weight of the branch. Some men had heard the crash and came running. They found Miccoon unresponsive but breathing and brought him here. Rohue tried to come and evoke the spirits for help, but I ran him off." Ona's face as she talked about Rohue was noticeably disgusted. "Toyuk, can you please pray to the Great Spirit for Miccoon, you too Tregor?" Ona gently asked.

"Of course, Ona." Toyuk kneeled down next to Miccoon and put his hand on Miccoon's head.

"Please be with Miccoon. Surround him with Your Presence, Great Spirit." Toyuk was praying quietly but Tregor and Ona could still hear him.

"I will be taking Miccoon home soon. He will come live with Me. His time is about over. There will be a celebration when he arrives home with Me." The Voice Toyuk was hearing in his head was the Voice of Jesus.

"Ona, has the Great Spirit told you anything?" Toyuk asked.

"Yes." Ona looked sad but wouldn't say anymore.

"Then you know."

"Yes."

Tregor looked back and forth between Toyuk and Ona, not yet understanding. Just then Miccoon opened his eyes and groaned.

"Miccoon, please stay still, we're here," Toyuk said gently.

Miccoon looked at Toyuk and then Tregor and smiled. Ona brought Miccoon some tea that helped with the pain. Then Ona helped Miccoon sip the tea. He lay back and closed his eyes. Tregor placed his hand on Toyuk's shoulder; Toyuk turned and shook his head. Tregor removed his hand thinking he had done the wrong thing. Toyuk immediately got up and went outside, and Tregor followed. When Tregor just walked out, Toyuk threw his arms around Tregor and held him tight. Tregor could feel Toyuk's silent sobbing convulsions.

After a long time holding on to Tregor, Toyuk spoke in a raspy voice, "Jesus said He will be taking Miccoon home soon."

Tregor was stunned and didn't know what to say because he had been thinking that the Great Spirit was just going to heal Miccoon and show everyone in the village His great power... again. Tregor couldn't find any words for Toyuk.

Nayee had walked over and saw Tregor holding Toyuk. "Does Ona need help?"

Tregor nodded for her to go in.

"May I help, Ona?" Nayee asked Ona quietly as she entered the dwelling.

"You can make some more tea." Ona pointed to the cooking fire.

Nayee set about crushing up some more herbs and seeds, placing them in the water of the stone bowl sitting near the small fire.

Tregor and Toyuk had then re-entered the dwelling quietly and were standing near the entrance.

Miccoon then stirred more and groaned. Then his eyes went wide and bright and he was looking up towards the ceiling, and a great smile was on his face.

"I see them! The warriors of our Chief Jesus are coming to take me with them!" Everyone's eyes were intently looking at Miccoon as he spoke. "They're wearing white skins that are shining bright. They look so powerful and strong. Oh... they're motioning to me...." Miccoon's voice trailed off and then he went silent.

Ona sobbed loudly. Toyuk grabbed Ona in a hug and sobbed with her. Tregor and Nayee put their arms around Ona and Toyuk. Nayee was surprised at Tregor as he began to speak.

"Great Spirit, thank you for taking our friend Miccoon to your home. Please be with us here now as we will greatly miss him. We need you to help us. I promise to take care of Ona now. Please help me do that now with honor."

"I agree, Jesus. Help us." Toyuk could be heard quietly in the middle of the group hug.

After a time of just being together without much talking, Nayee and Ona began preparing Miccoon's body. They wrapped the body with herbs in between the skins. Tregor and Toyuk had prepared the funeral stand for the firing of Miccoon's body.

The entire village that evening came to give honor to Miccoon. Rohue was noticeably absent. As Toyuk started the fire that consumed the body, many looked on and wept. That evening Toyuk had decided to sleep at Ona's dwelling. Ona and Toyuk talked much about the Great Spirit that evening, and how much it had settled Miccoon's heart in the past days. He had been so much more at peace than before. The real grief had not yet set in for Ona and Toyuk, because the shock of Miccoon's death was so sudden.

"I miss my mom, too," Toyuk said quietly.

"I've never felt that Shushe is dead... Toyuk. I think she is still alive and out there somewhere,"

Ona confessed to Toyuk.

Toyuk had pondered this for a while but hadn't ever discussed it with anyone. There was too much going on to address that issue in his heart. Sleep didn't come easy that night.

The next morning as the tribe was starting their day, Kinar announced that he would be making a decision that affected the entire tribe and wanted everyone at the village circle at midday. Once they had all gathered Kinar began speaking.

"We have had some big things affect our tribe that none of us could have seen. And those things have begun to divide us in ways that I do not think is good for the tribe. Because of our current status, I have made the decision that the Tregor family will be asked to leave this tribe and move far from us."

Immediately there was lots of talking among the tribe members, the division could be seen.

"All those who want to leave with the Tregor family will have to give tribute to the spirits and the tribe."

The talking got quieter.

"Rohue will be advising me as to the size of type of tribute needed from each family wanting to leave the tribe."

There were several who didn't like that idea but kept silent.

"The Tregor family must leave tomorrow. If you want to leave with them, Rohue will give you instructions as to your tribute that must be given." Kinar finished his statement and left the circle.

Rohue then approached Tregor. "Your tribute will be your bow." Rohue then turned to Toyuk.

"Your tribute will be Tonuw's knife," Rohue stated bluntly. "I will expect them this evening." Rohue turned and walked away.

"As always, Rohue gets rich off the tribe," Tregor said under his breath.

Toyuk was angry. He stormed off trying not to let his anger spill over onto anyone. He immediately began speaking to the Great Spirit. "Why is this so hard? Why do you allow Rohue and Kinar to do this? This will be difficult for Tregor, Nayee, and Nea. This will be hard on Ona. We just lost Miccoon. My mom isn't here." Toyuk was just rambling on, just talking and venting his anger and frustration. He hiked for quite a while and then just sat down.

"I know this is hard for you, but trust Me. I am with you. I will guide you. Now go back; Ona needs you."

Toyuk heard His Voice clearly in his head. Upon hearing that Ona needed him, Toyuk jumped up and ran towards the village.

Toyuk found Ona sitting alone in her dwelling just staring at nothing. "Ona, we need to begin to pack up what you want to take with you tomorrow." Ona said nothing and didn't respond. Toyuk began to speak out loud so Ona could hear him. "Jesus, forgive me. Forgive for being selfish and only thinking of myself, and my troubles. Jesus, please be with Ona now and comfort her. Great Spirit, envelope her with Your Presence." Toyuk could hear Ona quietly crying. "I'm here, Ona. I won't leave you," Toyuk said gently and quietly.

Nayee delivered the bow and knife for Tregor and Toyuk to Rohue. She said nothing but just dropped them in front of Rohue, turned and walked away.

Tregor and Nayee were packing up. Nea was helping her brother and sister pack their things.

Toyuk was helping Ona pack her things. Ona was giving away many things to other families as the Great Spirit guided her, even though she knew none would be leaving with her and the Tregor family. Toyuk was concerned for Ona as she seemed to be almost emotionless as she was working. She would often say under her breath, "Now is not the time," to herself.

So much was swirling in the mind of Toyuk. Tregor's family, Ona, Nea, and the next place, his own role in all of this, and what the future held. There was also this thing deep within him which he didn't know how to deal with—it wasn't something that the Holy Spirit warned him about, or corrected him on, or even explained, but it was there and growing. This deep void in his chest that he could feel, he didn't know what was happening to him. He finally stopped and asked the Holy Spirit what was this feeling that was growing inside of him.

The Holy Spirit said only one word: *"Grief."*

Toyuk knew instinctively that Ona was dealing with the same thing but on a much larger scale.

Please teach me how to deal with this, Toyuk was asking the Holy Spirit in his mind with real emotional angst.

"*Now you know how I feel*," was the response back from the Holy Spirit.

Toyuk was shocked and surprised. The Great Spirit, Jesus and the Father had these kinds of feelings and emotions? Why?

"*So many of my children have rejected Me, and I want to be so close to them, and help them. I love them, but they don't love me. I miss them.*"

The words rang in the heart of Toyuk from the Great Spirit. He was beginning in the smallest way to understand the void in his own heart currently missing Miccoon. These things made Toyuk ponder the deep mysteries of the Heart of the Great Spirit, Jesus, and the Father Creator. Toyuk found himself, as he worked, saying under his breath, "Now is not the time," and realized what Ona was doing, coping the best way she knew how.

Tregor was noticing that Nayee was reverting back to old ways, and her stern attitude and shortness towards those around her were much more evident. He pondered if it was the all the events of the past days, and how it was affecting her. He also knew the next days would not be easy. They would be physically hard, and uncomfortable. And he didn't know how many days they had ahead of them before they would ever get back to a normal life.

No one in the outcast group slept well that night.

18

A Long Walk

Toyuk and Tregor were up before the sun, packing all of their belongings onto the sleds they had constructed for the journey. Long poles with a skin and bindings held the baskets and other items that were pulled from behind. Plus, each individual had a pack on their back. Both Tregor and Toyuk would be pulling a sled.

Ona had given Tregor Miccoon's old bow and entire stash of arrows. Tregor had not seen Miccoon's bow as Miccoon's usual habits went to fishing for his meat. Miccoon's bow amazed Tregor; in fact he didn't want to admit that it was better than his own, that Rohue now had. He whispered his thanks to the Great Spirit as he realized these things.

Tregor knew Miccoon liked making arrows, and he began to understand that Miccoon was actually a very skilled marksman and craftsman. *So many things I should have explored with Miccoon if I hadn't been so wrapped up in my own problems.* Tregor was feeling the loss of Miccoon and the weight of his own past mistakes.

⇢——————⇢

The family and Ona set out north at first light. No one from the tribe had arrived to go with them. Tregor and Toyuk were pulling the sleds. Tregor led the way, then Nayee, Nea, and the two younger children, Ona, and then Toyuk at the back with another sled. The group of seven were headed to a place they did not know. But, at least for the first day, they were passing through known territory. Walking was slow and difficult with so much on their backs and sleds being pulled. At times Nayee had to pick up the back of Tregor's sled to get over certain rocks and difficult places. Nea helped Toyuk with his sled in those places. They stopped at every water source to fill up their water skins.

Tregor decided to stop early that first day so as not to wear everyone out too early. Setting up camp was slower than it should have been as everyone was grumpy and not used to the hard day of hiking. But Ona and Nayee had brought out food they had made beforehand that was rich with honey, and after eating everyone was feeling better. Nobody wanted to ask the questions that were on everyone's minds because they already knew the answer. No one knew how long they would be walking or how far their destination was. The conversation was mainly held to what was aching and how they felt physically.

To lighten everyone's mood, Tregor said that they should make it to the sacred valley in two more days and that they would camp there for the night. Toyuk had only heard stories about the sacred valley growing up, and Shushe had never let him explore places that far away. He had heard the stories from boys from their fathers who had taken them on the journey to see the magnificent sacred valley. But then it began to dawn on Toyuk what the sacred valley must be. He had been there before, it was called… Yosemite… in the time with the Petersons. They had visited the valley three times in the three years he had spent with them. He wondered what the valley looked like now. *I imagine it will be incredibly beautiful, especially without the roads, buildings, and people,* Toyuk thought to himself.

"Tregor, does the sacred valley have a massive rock that looks like half of it is gone on the eastern side of the valley? Does it have huge waterfalls and rock spires reaching high from the valley floor? Is the river that runs through the valley very beautiful?"

"I thought you had never been there, Toyuk?" Tregor was surprised at what Toyuk was describing.

"I think I have been there, Tregor, just not in this time. The family I lived with in the land of my dreams visited the valley three times while I lived with them."

"Three times?" Now Tregor was shocked and gave Toyuk some side eyes.

"It was just for a day."

"You must have walked for so long to visit the sacred valley just for a day?" Tregor was definitely puzzled and confused.

Toyuk knew that he would eventually have to tell people about his life in the other time. And now there were just seven of them who actually loved him.

"*Go ahead tell them*," came the response from the Holy Spirit in his mind.

"Tregor, we didn't walk to the valley. We traveled in a type of sled that pulled itself and could carry all of us at once. It was very fast."

Tregor's eyes were going wide. Everyone stopped as Toyuk began to share this information. Tregor knew Toyuk had stories about that time, but Toyuk had been very short on information about the things he experienced in that place.

"Would you be willing to tell us stories about that place and time, Toyuk?" Nea asked quietly. Everyone vigorously nodded in agreement.

Toyuk thought some. "Why don't I tell you a story about that time after supper every night till we get to the place the Great Spirit has chosen for all of us?"

Everyone liked that idea, but the younger children asked if Toyuk could tell his stories as they walked.

"I think we need to be very aware as we walk and not be distracted by stories," Toyuk responded.

"Toyuk is right," Tregor said. "In fact, we need to always be on the lookout for water sources and potential food along the way, and other dangers we might encounter—lions, bears, and other predators of the more dangerous type. We also must be very aware of where we step now, as you know that we will deal with snakes now. The tribe's warriors made sure the village area was clear of snakes as they would kill them if they got too close to the village."

Toyuk was enjoying hearing the fatherly wisdom coming from Tregor.

"We killed them too, Tregor." Ona was pointing at Nayee. "Miccoon loved their meat. He liked the way I prepared them. He also liked to use their skin for decoration on his items." Ona was pointing at the bow Miccoon had made.

"I would love to try your snake meat, Ona. But then there are snakes that we don't want to kill and those that we should just leave alone and only kill if we have to. I will make some snake sticks for anyone who wants one for our walking times." Tregor was talking to his younger children and already thinking he also needed to provide Ona with a good walking stick. "When we encounter a snake, it will be a good time to teach you younger ones what to look for," Tregor was instructing.

"You've already taught me some, and some of the other boys have already told me about some of the other kinds of snakes when we found them." Gnut was showing his father and everyone else that he was ready.

"I miss Miccoon," Nue, quietly said.

Toyuk grabbed the youngest daughter up in his arms and hugged her tight as he spun her around. When he stopped spinning, he whispered in her ear, "I do too, Nue. I think you should give Ona a hug as often as you can."

Nue nodded and smiled.

That night as they made their sleeping beds, Toyuk opened some of his skins and out dropped a knife. Miccoon's knife. He quickly looked directly at Ona. She nodded at him. Tears filled his eyes.

The seven were getting use to the daily walking, but Nayee had developed some blisters from the pack she was wearing. Some others as well had developed some sore areas from the hard traveling. Nayee had gotten more and more quiet as the days wore on. Gnut and Nue, though, were not having any difficulties with the walk but didn't like that they had to be so quiet as they walked.

Eventually they made it to the sacred valley. As they descended into the valley, they could see the cooking fires along certain portions of the river.

"We will have company," Tregor said cautiously.

"Tell us what to do, Tregor. We will follow your lead," Toyuk responded from the back of the pack.

"Start talking to the Great Spirit, Toyuk." Tregor looked back and pointed at him.

Toyuk nodded.

They had already passed several waterfalls that were bigger than any Nea or the younger children had ever seen. As they descended, they could see waterfalls that were the tallest and grandest they could have ever imagined.

"I can see why this is called the sacred valley." Nea was in awe at the beauty of the valley.

"We need to go to the eastern side of the valley, Tregor, past the great half rock," Toyuk called to Tregor who was in front pulling his sled.

Tregor nodded.

The seven avoided the fires and other camps as much as possible as they hiked north into the valley. It wasn't unusual to see others from other tribes in the sacred valley. Most just kept to themselves as they often had children with them who were being introduced to the valley for the first time.

"There was a history of those who tried to claim the valley as their own, but mostly those are bloody stories that never ended well for those who tried to make the valley off-limits to others," Tregor was quietly telling the group as they had found a secluded spot along the river and decided to set up camp for the night there.

"We want to hear Toyuk's stories," Gnut said a little louder than everyone would have liked.

The previous night Toyuk had told the story of his first night in that time, and encountering the flat rock path, and the flying stars close to the ground. Everyone was trying hard to see it in their heads while they listened. They tried to ask Toyuk questions, but he always said for them to just listen to the stories and he might answer their questions someday if they were patient because the future stories might give them answers to their questions.

That night after everyone had eaten, Toyuk decided to tell the story of when he climbed into a large dwelling type of sled that carried him and many, many others into the sky that flew higher than any bird could fly way above the clouds. Tregor was making faces like he didn't believe Toyuk, that the story wasn't a real story and that Toyuk was just making it up as a joke.

"All the stories I tell you are true. I will not lie or make up things. I know that these stories are unbelievable and hard to understand. They are hard for me to tell because they are hard to explain, as I don't have the words that you will understand. This is why I hesitate to tell these stories to others. The things the Great Spirit has allowed me to experience has made me understand that the Creator is so much more than we will ever know. And I know that Miccoon is now discovering some of those wonderful things in His land above."

"Thank you, Toyuk, for telling us your stories," Ona said with warmth.

Nea nodded, too.

"Tomorrow evening I will head into country I have not walked," Tregor said.

"Together we will all be on a new adventure," Toyuk said in agreement.

As they were getting ready to go to sleep, a man stumbled into their camp area and fell unconscious. He was bleeding from his side which looked like a wound from an arrow. When Toyuk and Tregor rushed over and turned the man over they both said "Leto." They motioned for Ona and Nayee to come. Ona brought her medicine basket. Ona had Nea get fresh water, and then she began to clean the wound and pack it with herbs. Nayee checked him for other wounds. Ona had Nayee start a tea for pain and healing. It wasn't too long and Leto regained consciousness, but remained still. When Ona saw that he was awake, she motioned Tregor over. Toyuk remained on lookout for any others.

"What happened to you, Leto? Why are you here?" Tregor was sternly looking at Leto.

"Tribe ...attacked. Many dead. Most ran for their lives. I ran to this valley. Thinking I should have left with you." Leto was having difficulty getting the words out.

"Were there others that followed you?" Tregor was thinking about the safety of his family.

"I don't know. I ran as fast as I could. Can I have some water?"

Ona brought the water skin to Leto. Nayee brought the tea and handed it to Leto. Tregor got up to go talk to Toyuk.

"Leto says the tribe was attacked and that many are dead," said Tregor. " He doesn't know if any followed him."

Toyuk pondered this information from Tregor. "Someone needs to be on watch tonight. I'll take first watch." Toyuk had his bow ready with an arrow notched.

"I will go back and see if Leto has any more information."

Nayee and Ona slipped aside to discuss Leto's condition. Nea stayed with Leto.

"He's lost a lot of blood, and he's pretty weak." Nayee was almost in a whisper.

"I think he's also bleeding inside, and one of his major organs may have been punctured," Ona replied quietly.

"What do we do?" Nayee was watching Nea and Leto as she said this.

"I don't think he'll make it through the night, Nayee." Ona was shaking her head.

Tregor then arrived back just in time to hear Ona's last words to Nayee. "I think Toyuk needs to talk to Leto about the Great Spirit and His Son Jesus right now."

Ona and Nayee nodded. Tregor got up and picked up Miccoon's old bow and arrows and went to trade places with Toyuk.

"How are you my old friend?" Toyuk was kneeling next to Leto. Nea was putting a cold skin on Leto's forehead.

"I've been better."

"You ran a long way just to get here. Why Leto? Why us?" Toyuk was gentle in his words.

"That night you told your story, I believed you. I believed your stories about the Great Spirit and His son. Then with the arrows and target? No one could have made those shots, but both Nea and Ona did? Impossible. I knew you had the Great Spirit's help. And then Nea's leg? I so wanted to go with all of you, but I just ...." Leto was fading and slowing.

"It's okay, Leto. I'm here. The Great Spirit knows your heart. Do you believe in the work Jesus did for all of us?"

"Yes." Leto's reply was soft and weak.

"Just lie still. Great Spirit, be with Leto now." Toyuk was talking quietly to Leto and praying.

Nea just watched. Ona and Nayee came to Leto and covered him with a fur. They also came and kneeled by Toyuk, and Nea got up to be with Gnut and Nue.

Leto had his eyes closed and breathing was more labored. "Will you please pray and ask the Great Spirit what we should do?"

Toyuk was looking at Ona and Nayee. Both nodded. Toyuk got up to walk and pray. He scanned the area as he walked.

Great Spirit, what is it you want to do? Do you want Leto to live here or be with You? What is it You want us to do? We want to agree with You Great Spirit.

"*Leto will soon be with Me. I've sent My warriors to escort him here. Miccoon is waiting to receive and greet Leto. Toyuk, keep praying for Leto; he's scared, but his fear will soon be joy.*"

The Holy Spirit was gentle and calm in the mind of Toyuk.

Toyuk slowly walked back to Leto. "The Great Spirit is with you, Leto. He loves you. He tells me you will be with Him soon. He has sent His warriors to escort you to Him. He also said that Miccoon is waiting there to see you. Don't be afraid."

At this both Nayee and Ona looked at Toyuk. Toyuk just half smiled in response.

What happened next was something no one of their group had seen before. A slight white glow began to surround Leto. Leto stirred, and raised his arms out at something, and then just fell back. The glow was gone. Leto had breathed his last.

Tregor by now figured no one had followed Leto. But he was still cautious. Toyuk came beside Tregor. "Let's get Gnut to stand watch. I'm pretty sure no one else followed him. Let's build a shorter funeral stand for Leto and fire his body tonight before it attracts predators."

Tregor nodded and they went to work finding the branches and wood. Ona and Nayee prepared Leto's body. They all soon stood and watched the fire consume the body of Leto. The funeral stand was a distance from their camp. Gnut was in charge of watching the camp and "helping" keep Ona safe as she put things away.

It was much later by the time everyone could sleep. Toyuk still wanted to keep watch. Tregor told him he would take over after he slept some. Toyuk pondered all the things that had happened in the past weeks. He slipped into his regular conversation mode with the Great Spirit.

Great Spirit, what happened at our village? Is there anyone left? Where do you want us to go?

Where do you want to lead us? Toyuk had so many questions.

"The place I have for you is still four days north of here. There will be two lakes and a river between them. It is a good and plentiful area. The people that were once there are no more.

Everyone thinks the area is filled with bad spirits, so no one ventures there. The family will be safe there. On your fourth day of walking, I will show you where to turn." The Holy Spirit was very clear and concise but didn't answer any other of Toyuk's questions.

A time later Tregor came and Toyuk went to get some sleep.

The morning seemed to come earlier for the family, as everyone had been up late the night before. They were slow in packing up, and it was decided that they would just eat corn cakes on the walk out of the valley.

They were slowly finding their way along and over mountain ridges. Each night they resumed having Toyuk tell a story from his time away. These stories were hard to believe and hard to imagine what things really must have looked like in that place. But Gnut, Nue, and Nea were fascinated by the stories and loved them. Ona just marveled and pondered the work of the Great Spirit.

Nayee was troubled by the information Leto had brought. She was thinking about so many from the tribe that she had been friends with. What had happened to them? Where were they now? She wondered about the fate of Rohue and Kinar. The hate she had for those two was still festering in her heart. Tregor could tell that Nayee was still struggling with something but didn't know if he should talk to her about it.

On the fourth day of walking, Toyuk was leading with Tregor taking the back. Toyuk had shared with Tregor the instructions the Great Spirit had shared with him. As Toyuk looked at the tall rock faces on a mountain ahead, he heard the Holy Spirit.

"Turn down this ridge. Find the river. Go past the first lake, your new home is between the two lakes. You'll find the grinding rock." Toyuk motioned to the left with his arm, and the group took a left turn down the ridge.

19

A New Beginning

It was midafternoon when they approached the first lake, they stopped to look at it and could see it was a pretty good-sized lake with lots of good camping spots around it.

"Let's camp here, I'm tired," Nue said quietly.

"Nue, the Great Spirit says our new home will be on the river just beyond this lake, don't you want to get there so we don't have any more days of walking?" Toyuk asked Nue. "At least it's all downhill from here."

"I guess," Nue said slowly with tiredness in her voice.

"Nue, please walk with me, I need your help." Ona was reaching out to Nue.

"I'm proud of you, Nue. You are the youngest one here, and you've kept up with us. This is the first time I've heard you complain. You are doing great! I know you can make it." Tregor was giving Nue praise, because he really was proud of her. The Holy Spirit had been working on Tregor's heart towards his children and to be more open with them as well as praise them when he saw them doing well at a task he had asked them to do. Nayee had also been seeing the good subtle changes in Tregor as well, but she was too involved with her own issues to say anything to Tregor.

"Can I walk with you?" Gnut asked Toyuk.

Toyuk looked at Tregor. Tregor nodded. "Sure Gnut, why don't you lead the way and find the easiest path for us. Be sure not to get too far out ahead." Toyuk was starting to see Gnut as a younger brother and was proud of how Gnut was always eager to learn more from him.

"Have your bow ready," Toyuk instructed.

Gnut nodded and walked ahead. So far Gnut had actually done really well charting the path for the group. He was mindful of the sleds both Toyuk and Tregor were pulling and the space they needed.

It was late afternoon when they arrived at a place where the river slowed and widened out, with lots of open spaces around it. There were the remnants of an old village about a hundred paces on one the higher open areas. There were good grinding holes near the river. And to the south of the village area lots of rich, flat ground that would be a great vegetable growing area. The group was in awe of how this place was so perfect, yet no one was there. Ona and Nayee were pointing and talking about all the plans they had when looking around the new place. Nea was at the river soaking her feet and washing the dirt off her legs. Nue no longer seemed tired as she and Gnut were running from place to place. Tregor and Toyuk began making camp.

"This place looks so good!" Tregor was looking around.

"I have something to share with the entire group that the Great Spirit told me when He spoke about this place," said Tuyok.

Tregor tilted his head when he heard this. "After we're done eating, let's sit as a family and discuss. Now let's get a fire going," Tregor said.

After the family had eaten, Tregor made an announcement.

"Toyuk has something to say." Ona and Nayee stopped and listened before putting everything away.

Toyuk began speaking slowly, "When the Great Spirit told me about this place, He gave the reason why no one is here. It is believed by those around this greater area that bad spirits live here, so no one ventures to come here. The Great Spirit said we would be safe here." Nue hugged Ona close as Toyuk talked about the bad spirits. Nayee looked at Tregor.

"I think we should give the Great Spirit thanks for leading us here, for protecting us, and blessing us. We should thank Him for getting all of us here safely," Tregor said with confidence.

Toyuk then began to speak loudly, thanking the Great Spirit for His protection, direction, and blessings. Tregor followed. Soon everyone had thanked the Great Spirit openly and loudly. The group went about getting ready to sleep by making places around the fire.

Of course, Gnut and Nue asked for a story from Toyuk.

Toyuk thought about what story he would tell. He then began trying to figure out how to explain. . . television. Everyone had furrowed brows on their faces as they tried to understand the "black flat rock" which could show places and people as Toyuk was trying to explain.

After the children were asleep, Tregor pulled Toyuk aside. "I think we need to keep watch this first night. Something isn't setting right in me. I sense that there is something out there."

Toyuk was quiet when he heard what Tregor had said. He paused and listened. "I agree. My spirit is uneasy for some reason."

Tregor and Toyuk sat together with their bows ready as the stars shone, and moon rose in the cloudless sky. They were in between the river and their camp about fifty paces away so they wouldn't disturb anyone's sleep. They both sat silently scanning the area, looking, watching, waiting for what they didn't know.

Tregor saw it first, as a shadow moving on the other side of the river. "I think it's a wolf," he whispered to Toyuk as they both silently stood up.

"Then there'll be more of them." Toyuk whispered back.

"Maybe. Get ready," replied Tregor.

All of sudden, just twenty paces ahead of them, was a snarling wolf. Immediately both had their bows pointed at the wolf. Then something happened which Toyuk couldn't explain. It was like time slowed down and he heard the Holy Spirit clearly in his head speaking and giving him instructions.

This is not an ordinary wolf. This wolf is inhabited by an evil spirit. Do not kill it because it will set the spirit to look for another to inhabit. Speak to the spirit and loudly say this, "In the Name of Jesus be gone. Leave this place. Do not come back. Never return. I command you in the Name of Jesus, Son of God."

All of these instructions and words only took a fraction of time to be said in Toyuk's mind. Toyuk reached out and moved Tregor's bow down, and at the same time said the exact words the Holy Spirit had told him to say. Tregor began to say something but Toyuk had already begun speaking to the evil spirit in the wolf. Tregor watched in fascination as the wolf whimpered and trotted off.

"Well, that was new," Toyuk said after both looked at one another. "I'm still learning. I think my Bible says something about this, I will have to seek it out in the book."

"Yes, that *was* new," Tregor was looking amazed at Toyuk.

"What was it you said Jesus was the Son of Who?" Tregor was remembering what Toyuk had said to the wolf.

"God. It's from the language of the other place the Great Spirit took me to; it's what they call the Great Spirit there."

"Well, it worked. I've never seen a wolf do that before from just speaking to it."

"The Holy Spirit told me that an evil spirit inhabited the body of the wolf, and that I needed to command it to leave the area, and not to kill it because then the spirit would look for another to inhabit."

"I think there is more for us to learn, Toyuk." Tregor was clearly interested in learning more about the spirit realm.

The next morning the group was excited and talking to one another. They were exploring the old dwellings and surrounding area. Tregor had said that he and Toyuk would dismantle and take down the old dwellings but use some of the materials for the new ones. Gnut was trying his hand at fishing, trying to remember all the lessons he had learned from Miccoon. Soon he stood up in the river with a fish in his hand.

"Well done, Gnut! Now clean it for your mother," Tregor called out to him.

Nue and Nea were returning from the future garden area with baskets in their arms.

"We found a few corn stalks, some dried cobs, and some good root vegetables," Nea was telling Nayee and Ona.

"That's wonderful," Ona replied as she looked in the baskets.

Toyuk was returning with a rabbit he had just shot.

"Meat for Gnut's hungry stomach." Toyuk raised the rabbit in the air.

"The boy is already providing us with fish!" Tregor pointed Toyuk towards the river proudly.

"Go, Gnut!!!" Toyuk shouted at Gnut.

Gnut just smiled inside, he was focused on catching fish number two.

The midday cooking fire was smelling really good from fresh roasting rabbit and freshly caught fish.

Everyone was feeling very satisfied when Nea asked Toyuk a question. "I heard you last night speaking loudly. Who were you speaking to?"

Tregor then told the story of what happened last night with the lone wolf. And Toyuk restated the exact words the Holy Spirit has instructed him to say.

"This place actually may be a place where bad spirits were allowed to roam freely. But no more. The Holy Spirit is teaching me how to take care of bad spirits with the Name of Jesus." Everyone was listening with seriousness.

"You are becoming quite the experienced Shaman, Toyuk," Ona plainly stated.

"Ona, I'm not sure that I'm a Shaman. All of you have the same Holy Spirit living inside of you; I'm no different than you when it comes to hearing and obeying Him. Nea, Ona, remember the arrows?" Toyuk was looking at both Nea and Ona. "And I've been thinking a lot lately about our family, our new tribe. And I think Tregor should be our chief."

Tregor's eyes went wide at Toyuk's statement and then he closed them for a long time. The others waited for him to respond. When Tregor finally opened his eyes, he began to speak slowly. "I'm not sure I'm worthy to be chief. I've made so many mistakes in the past."

"Tregor, we all have made many mistakes. But Jesus asks us to ask Him for forgiveness. Then He leads us to make right what we can with others. I got so angry at Rohue and Kinar when they conspired to get us kicked out of the tribe and turn everyone against us. The Holy Spirit has been asking me to forgive them. I'm still trying to do that. It's not easy. My anger led me away while Ona needed my help. I was selfish." Toyuk was sharing from deep places within him.

"I... too... have much hatred for Kinar and Rohue," Nayee said firmly. "They stole my husband's place, joy, respect, and confidence. Rohue stole my daughter's hair!" Nayee was getting louder. "They turned our friends against us." Nayee kept going. "I don't know if I will EVER forgive them!"

Nayee was now shouting.

Ona moved to sit with Nayee and just put her arm around her. Toyuk began asking the Holy Spirit what to do.

Begin by asking Me for forgiveness for the mistakes you made that I bring to your mind in front of everyone here.

Toyuk began to speak out loud to the Great Spirit, confessing every mistake the Great Spirit was reminding him of, and asking the Great Spirit's forgiveness. After Toyuk had finished, there was a long silence. Then Tregor began confessing before the Great Spirit and asking the Great Spirit for forgiveness for not being a good chief, husband, father, and friend. Then Ona began praying out loud, thanking the Great Spirit for leading all of them in His ways, and teaching them all how to be humble and ask forgiveness quickly. Nea began thanking the Great Spirit for her healed leg but also for healing her heart, and helping her find joy again, and for blessing her with such a great father and mother. Toyuk then began to pray again.

"Father, I pray for Kinar, Rohue, and Buldar, that You would show yourself to them. Help them know You and Your Son Jesus. I forgive them, Great Spirit, for all the bad things they did and wanted to do to me."

"Yes, Great Spirit, I forgive them," Ona spoke clearly and quietly.

"Great Spirit, I, too, ask that You help me forgive them in my heart, for only You know how much I hated them," Tregor said quietly.

Nayee listened to Tregor's honesty that he needed the Great Spirit's help in forgiving them. "Me, too," was all Nayee could say very quietly.

Toyuk came over to Nayee and put his arms around her.

"That's all the Great Spirit wants, Nayee. Honesty from us. That's all He requires from us. He gives us the abilities and power we don't have to do what He asks us to do. Remember Nea and Ona and the arrows? There's no way they could do those things without Him. The same thing I need in forgiving Kinar and Rohue."

Nayee nodded and was quietly crying.

"Shaman. Toyuk," Ona said teasingly. Everyone laughed, even Nayee.

"Well, I'm certain who I want as my Chief of this Tribe and it's Tregor!" Toyuk stated loudly and went to give Tregor a hug.

"Fine," Tregor said to Toyuk, and threw up his arms like he was giving up. "Everyone must agree here, I'm not accepting the role if anyone has any doubts."

Everyone started telling Tregor they wanted him as their Chief.

"Fine. Fine. Then I'll accept the role of Chief if Toyuk accepts the role of our tribe's Shaman." Tregor looked squarely at Toyuk.

"Well, you know he has my vote." Ona smirked. Tregor laughed. Nayee laughed too.

"I'm a little too young to be the tribe's Shaman," Toyuk was looking for a way out.

"No, you're not. The Chief has spoken." Tregor laughed.

"I'm not using the title. It doesn't mean the same thing anymore to me." Toyuk was still trying to get out of the use of the title.

"The title isn't what's important, Toyuk, it's what you do—your gifts and your purpose in this family. We see the Great Spirit's purpose in you, Toyuk. Miccoon saw it. I see it in you now. I've seen it for a long time." Ona was speaking eloquently and with the force of the Holy Spirit.

"I see it," Tregor said solemnly.

"So do I," Nayee confirmed.

"Yes. Me... too," said Nea.

Toyuk looked at everyone. He was internally having a conversation with the Great Spirit. Everyone could see Toyuk was wrestling with something inside him. "Then I will try to do the hardest thing I have ever attempted." Toyuk paused. Everyone waited, wondering what Toyuk was referring to. No one could have guessed what Toyuk would say next. "Officially ...I ask the Chief of this tribe for the hand of his daughter to be my wife," Toyuk said slowly, looking at Nea instead of Tregor.

Ona started a warrior yell. Gnut and Nue joined in. Nea blushed. Nayee jumped up and threw her arms around Toyuk and started jumping up and down. After everyone stopped celebrating, Tregor spoke. "It would be my highest honor to accept your proposal, Toyuk," Tregor said in his best Chief voice.

"Does this mean I get to marry Toyuk?" Nue asked, smiling. "I mean Toyuk didn't say which ... daughter."

Everyone laughed.

"And since you all say I have the role of you-all-know-what, I can't marry us myself, so I officially appoint Ona to take this role and honor. Tregor, you know it's the you-know-what's role to do the ceremony."

"Oh... I've been waiting for this. It is happening tonight, right?" Nayee was looking at Tregor with great joy on her face.

"I think Nayee is right. Tonight, we prepare for a wedding under the moon," Tregor announced.

"Oh... I have so much to do. So many things to ask the Great Spirit. So much to prepare for." And Ona quickly set off walking and almost skipping in another direction.

"Me, too." And Nayee set off dancing to where all of her supplies were.

There was so much activity going on. Tregor had taken Gnut and Toyuk hunting for dinner. Amazingly they were able to kill a buck quicker than Tregor had ever experienced before in his life. In just a short time the three had skinned and cut up the meat back at their new village area. While the men were hunting, Nayee had called Nea and Ona over and the three were deep into conversation and plans. Once the men returned, Ona had gotten out spices and things she hadn't pulled out on the entire journey to their new home. Nayee also was utilizing things Tregor hadn't seen on the entire trip.

The night's dinner was a grand affair. Everyone was laughing and enjoying the bounty of their new home. Then as soon as it was done, they quickly cleaned up and went their separate ways. Nayee, Ona, Nea, and Nue went to one end of the camp and had put up several skins so that they couldn't be seen. Tregor, Toyuk and Gnut went to the other side of their camp. Tregor got out some white skins from deep in a pack. Toyuk had never seen Tregor's white skins before.

"These I wore on my wedding night with Nayee. Now you should wear them."

Toyuk was amazed at the craftsmanship, and the ornate beading and coloring on the skins. "I'm so honored by you, Tregor."

Toyuk didn't know exactly what to say. He didn't really get to be a part of weddings when he was a boy, or even in his time with the Petersons. This wedding thing was new to him. He had seen some weddings when he was smaller but only from a distance.

"I am blessed and honored by the Great Spirit to have you join this family officially." Tregor's voice was raspy as emotion was overwhelming him.

"Gnut, will you stand beside me?" Toyuk asked.

"It would be my honor," Gnut said with as much of an adult voice he could muster. Gnut was so happy to have Toyuk now officially as a big brother.

On the other side of their camp the women were preparing Nea. Ona and Nayee had gotten out their wedding skins and presented them to Nea for her to use. Nea was overwhelmed and didn't want to disappoint either of them. With their help they figured out how to include parts of both into what she would wear for the ceremony. Nue had run off to gather flowers. She then set about weaving a crown of flowers with the help of Ona for Nea's head. Ona, Nayee, and Nue then themselves all got dressed for the occasion.

Tregor had walked over and from the other side of the skins asked if they were ready.

"Just give us some time please. We'll all be ready in a bit." Nayee responded in such a way Tregor knew not to push it any further.

Tregor walked back to Toyuk and Gnut. Tregor and Gnut had on the best skins they had with them. Toyuk was surprised because Tregor had on some chieftain skins he hadn't seen in a long time.

Toyuk was wearing the white skins Tregor had given him. Gnut had Miccoon's knife at his side, as he had asked Toyuk if he could borrow it for the ceremony. And they waited on a large flat stone near the river easily seen by the camp.

Soon the procession began with Nue holding flowers walking in front, followed by Ona who was wearing a very complex, ornate, and beautiful deer skin that flowed to the ground, and then Nayee wearing a beautiful skin and also holding flowers. Then came Nea in white skins that Tregor and Toyuk could have never expected. On her head she wore a crown of flowers. She took both of Tregor's and Toyuk's breaths away.

Toyuk gulped. The Holy Spirit gave him encouragement.

Hold it together, Toyuk. See what I'm blessing you with?

"Great Spirit, we are here to give You honor and praise…" Ona began speaking once they were all on the large rock by the river as she stood in front of Toyuk and Nea.

20

One Year Later

"Hey, Brent, how's the burgers coming?" Erik was checking his smoker that had two tri-tips cooking.

"Ask Stephanie if she's got the cheese ready, I want to melt some on." Brent was on the BBQ moving some burgers to a higher shelf on the grill.

"You got it, brother." Erik was headed back into the kitchen.

"Kathy said she was also bringing a three-bean salad." Stephanie was talking to Diana. Diana was putting her green salad on the counter.

"Hey, Hun, you got the cheese ready for the burgers? Brent's ready for it."

"Yep, on the counter ready to go."

Just then Bethany walked into the kitchen from the garage carrying two homemade apple pies. "Brought some pies, Mom. Not sure it will be enough."

"Don't worry, Hun, Karin said she's bringing some pumpkin pies from the store," Stephanie said, taking the pies from her daughter.

"Do you have ice cream?"

"We've got the ice cream maker going on the patio," Erik answered Bethany as he was walking out with the cheese.

"YES! Score!" Bethany raised her fist in the air.

It was a usual Saturday night at the Peterson ranch—a big potluck with all the best their friends and families could muster. Bethany had moved out a year ago and was living in an apartment with her best friend Hannah from school. She had taken a job as a server in a local downtown restaurant in Clovis and was working on her art. Michael was away at college headed into his master's program.

After the potluck they all moved into the Peterson barn for a time of worship and sharing. Life had changed for Erik and Stephanie over the past year since Toyuk had just disappeared from their lives. Erik had left his volunteer chaplain position at the hospital, and Stephanie was busier than ever running a small homeschool network, as so many parents had now withdrawn their children from the public school system. And they had left their church and started a different style of fellowship in their barn.

After Erik and Stephanie finally finished the cleanup of the potluck, they walked to the barn and could both hear that the worship music was already going. People were sitting on hay bales, benches, and chairs in various places. There was no formal set up of chairs where people sat other than a kind of circle was arranged. A young man named David was strumming his guitar in the back and singing, and many people were singing along with him. As Erik and Stephanie entered, they were greeted by Mark who came up and gave them a hug. David had stopped playing and Bob had started praying, thanking, and welcoming the Holy Spirit to be with everyone.

After Bob's prayer, Mark asked if there was anyone that wanted to share anything the Lord had given them in the past week.

"This is not like me, at least it wasn't usual for me, but I'll share something." Erik was starting and stopping.

Mark could tell Erik wasn't very confident. "Go ahead, brother, we're with you," Mark encouraged Erik.

"Well, I've been spending time in the morning with the Lord, um... that's not new, but um... listening to the Holy Spirit for whatever He wanted to tell me... is something I'm learning. And that I'm actually getting something that's ... not really normal for me... is kind of different, but I can tell it's Him." Erik was struggling to find the words to say. "But here goes... it's a kind of psalm of a personal nature. I begin to write the words I hear in my heart and spirit or mind or ... I don't know which... anyway ...."

Erik began to read from a journal he had pulled out.

"The storm rages without

Father, You are my refuge and my hiding place
I seek you when I rise
Whispering thanks for life and Your love
"The enemy shouts and sneers
Wisdom is maligned
Understanding is rejected
Truth is scorned
Shame is thrown like dung at my head
They hate You, spewing vile lies
Twisting every word into knives
"O Lord—I seek Your help
Help me with my spiritual armor
Teach me how to fight, O Captain
Your ways fortify my shield
Sharpen my sword—that I might hear Your Word
"Instruct me in the path
Holy Spirit, illumine my steps forward
Breathe into me—For You are my life and power
Drench me in Your Presence
"Jesus, I draw near to YouMeet me with Your embrace
Your friendship is so precious to me
Your Voice is a balm to my heart and soul
Lead me in ...Jesus."
Erik stopped reading.

"Wow. Erik, that really blessed me. I'm going to want a copy of that." Mark was so impressed and moved by the inspiration from the Holy Spirit coming through Erik. He marveled at the growth he had seen in Erik over the past year, as Erik pushed into learning to hear the Holy Spirit.

"I've got something. The Lord has been giving me some music and words," Charlene spoke up. She then went to her electronic piano she had just unrolled and began to play and sing.

"Come away with me, my beloved
Come away and talk with Me awhile

Let your burdens roll off your shoulders
Come away, My bride
Come away with me, My beloved
Come away and walk with Me awhile
Let your head rest on My shoulders
Come away, My bride, My beloved
"Let go of your fear… I'm holding you tight
Step into My yoke … My burden is light
My yoke is easy … walk in step with me
I am gentle … just trust and rest in Me
"Take my doubt, my sin, my pain
Banish fear and wash away my shame
Teach me, Lord, how to be, not do
Show me, Lord, how to rest in You
"Come away, come away, come and walk with Me, My bride
Come away my beloved, trust and rest in Me, My bride
"I trust You, I'll rest in You
Every day I'll walk and talk with You
I've nothing to fear, nothing to hide
For You walk with me side by side
My Beloved, You're my Beloved."

Little by little others joined her on the chorus. Cordell had picked up an empty plastic five-gallon bucket, turned it over and began drumming to the beat. Cordell's young daughters were dancing and swaying to the music. And then David joined in on his guitar. David's young son had joined Cordell's daughters in the dance. People were worshiping in all different postures. Bob was raising his arms and hands. His eyes were closed, and he was singing along. Some were kneeling. Some had their hands over their faces.

"Bob looks like a skyscraper," Bethany whispered to Stephanie.

Bob, the former basketball player, was by far the tallest in the group. His wife Charlene was singing and on the piano. When Charlene had finished, everyone was overwhelmed with His Presence and Hallelujahs were heard and praises to God throughout the group.

"That was SO good, Charlene," Stephanie said so everyone could hear.

"I've got something I'd like to say." A woman from the back spoke up and waved her hand.

"Cindy, is that you?" Erik thought he recognized the voice. He knew her as a nurse at the hospital where he had volunteered.

"Yep," came the reply.

"I know Erik from the hospital. I was a nurse there." Cindy was saying as she stood up and stepped to the front edge of the circle. "I too left the hospital just after Erik did. I couldn't go through with the mandate of required experimental gene therapy shots. I'm exploring, researching, and learning about local plant based natural medicines now. Kathy, Mark's wife, had me come tonight. I'm pretty new at all this spiritual stuff. But I gave my heart to Jesus and the next thing I know I'm out of a job and being led in a different direction. But then there was this strange man who walked up to me and gave me a word he said he got from the Lord. Boy, he's strange." Cindy winked at Mark. "So here I am saying that … well… Jesus is my life now, and I'm learning what that kind of means as I am learning from the Holy Spirit. You know, Mark, your Holy Spirit boot camp with Cordell and your coaching is helping me a lot." Cindy was looking at Mark and folding her hands in thanks towards both Mark and Cordell.

"Welcome, Cindy! Hey, see me afterwards. I'm really interested in your natural medicine research." Erik had walked over to Cindy after she had finished.

And that's how it usually went—a night of sharing and fellowship. Everyone was getting used to nights going long; people just didn't want them to end. The Presence of the Holy Spirit in the barn and the people just felt so … real. The formal three songs and a sermon style from the regular 'Church service' days had been abandoned for allowing the Holy Spirit to move as He saw fit within the group. On the Saturday night fellowship meeting the group knew to bring what they had been receiving from the Lord throughout the week.

Of course, there were weekly teaching times, but they were in different groups and different days. Stephanie had a weekly women's group Bible study. Erik had a men's group meeting every week on Thursday nights at 7pm which tended to move around as the Spirit led. There was no formal paid minister or pastor within the group, just elder types who followed the leading of the Holy Spirit.

"You all are invited tomorrow around ten for brunch and an afternoon of games. Bob, you bringing your famous wild pig bacon and sausage? Doug will be bringing the farm fresh eggs. Sherrie will be bringing her goat cheese. And I think Bob is going to provide some great target practice coaching to those who want to shoot. Ted, are you bringing your corn hole game?" Ted nodded while Erik was pointing at several men. "And, of course, Stephanie will have the croquet tournament going on the lawn. So, anyone who wants to just hang out together tomorrow, we'll be here. Mark, why don't you close out our time tonight in prayer." Erik motioned to Mark.

Things had definitely changed for Erik and Stephanie. It wasn't long after Toyuk's disappearance that Erik had called Mark to get together for lunch. That turned into a three-hour lunch discussion, which led to dinner the next night at Mark and Kathy's home where the four of them had so much to talk about. The friendship quickly clicked for all of them, and the two couples began what became the Saturday night worship and sharing time with the Sunday family game day.

Mark was working part time with Brent and his son David in their small pool plumbing and electrical business whose families also became part of the small Peterson "barn tribe" as it began to be known. The barn tribe meetings usually only had twenty to twenty-five people in attendance. The goal was never big numbers of people, but the goal was the Presence of the Holy Spirit and His life in the group. Mark was also working on writing and holding boot camps of the Holy Spirit's nature where true followers of Christ could learn to hear the Voice of the Holy Spirit and grow and be taught by Him.

"The evidence of the Holy Spirit is the FRUIT of Jesus being developed in the character of the person," one could always hear Mark saying.

Character Index

Toyuk

(Beginning of book age 14)
Boy
Son of Shushe
Good at hand fishing
Faster runner than Buldar (Best Friend)
Has a good ability to remember places
Has good hand eye coordination
Thin build, smaller than the average boy his age
Voice is changing at beginning

Buldar

(Same age as Toyuk)
Boy
Best friend of Toyuk
Terrible at fishing
More athletic build than Toyuk

Very good at wrestling
Uncle is Growlon

Shushe

Woman
Single mom of Toyuk – Age early 30's
Husband killed while she was pregnant

Tonuw

Toyuk's father now dead.

Miccoon

Man
Tribal Elder – Age 60's
Married to Ona
No children
In charge of fishing trial for manhood initiation
Wants to "adopt" Toyuk

Ona

Woman
Married to Miccoon- Age late 50's
No children
Expert Basket maker
Known for her designs

Treats Shushe like a daughter
Believes in the "Great Spirit" who is the creator and ruler of all
Has dreams

Nea

Girl friend of Toyuk – Age 14
Grew up with Toyuk
Facing womanhood initiation
Highly prized as a potential mate
Long black hair
Is being possibly sought as a mate for Kinar
Father is TregorMother is Nayee

Tregor

Man
Tribal Leader – Age Mid to late 30's
Father of Nea
In charge of archery initiation area
Very concerned with maintaining high status in the tribe
Tribe's best hunter, inventor and builder of traps
Not encouraging Nea to pursue a continuing friendship with Toyuk
Not warm towards Toyuk in the beginning of the book

Leto

Boy
Same age as Toyuk
Likes to talk

Gets in trouble for gossiping
Is somewhat shunned by other boys

Yellot

Boy
A year older than Toyuk
Passed over last years initiation ritual
Big, chubby, somewhat quiet
Not a warrior type
Likes wrestling

Rohue

Late 40's
Man
The tribal Shaman

Erik Peterson

Mid 40's
Man

Stephanie Peterson

Early 40's
Woman / wife of Erik
Public 3rd grade schoolteacher

Michael Peterson

17 yrs old Beginning
Skinny / Smart
Older brother to Bethany
In the 'group' at school

Bethany Peterson

14 yrs old beginning
Younger sister to Michael
On the outs with the cool crowd

Manvir Singh

Friend and classmate of Michael's

Joe

Friend of Michael's

Mark

Mysterious prophet-like man, older, glasses, beard

Nayee

Age early 30's
Woman
Wife of Tregor
Mother of Nea

Gnut

Boy / son of Tregor and Nayee
Younger brother of Nea
7 years old Beginning of book / 10 after

Nue

Girl / daughter of Tregor and NayeeYoungest child
6 years old beginning of book, 9 after

Kinar

Single Male looking for a wife -age 18 at beginning / 21 after
Has high status in tribe
Is very good looking – has long black hair
Very prideful
Strong warrior
Has eyes on Nea for Wife
Is negotiating with Tregor for Nea

Growlon

Man
Tribal Leader – Age Late 30's
Has killed 3 grizzlies – wears three claws around neck
Best in tribe in hand to hand combat
In charge of hand to hand area in initiation ritual
Uncle to Buldar
Not tall – but very wide athletic muscular build

About the Author

Joseph was given a terminal diagnosis early in life with only six months to live. After opting out of all therapies, Joseph was healed by Jesus in a single day. The term "Terminally Committed to Christ" began with that experience. TC² is a response to the call of Jesus to take up one's cross and follow Him with the promise that those who lose their lives for His sake shall find new life in Him–"for it is no longer I who live, but Christ who lives in me."

Connect with J. Pauls online **(feel free to send him your questions or comments):**
Website & Blog: www.terminallycommitted.com
Instagram: @terminallycommitted

www.ingramcontent.com/pod-product-compliance
Lightning Source LLC
Chambersburg PA
CBHW072136300726

48975CB00003B/1084